Rebecca and Rowena

William Makepeace Thackeray

ET REMOTISSIMA PROPE

100 PAGES

100 PAGES

Published by Hesperus Press Limited

4 Rickett Street, London sw6 1RU

www.hesperuspress.com

First published 1850

First published by Hesperus Press Limited, 2002

Foreword © Matthew Sweet, 2002

Designed and typeset by Fraser Muggeridge

Printed in the United Arab Emirates by Oriental Press

ISBN: 1-84391-018-7

CONTENTS

Queen Victoria's coronation was done on the cheap. The Whig government declined to pay for the full complement of pomp and circumstance, and Archibald William Montgomerie, Earl of Eglinton, was among those most crestfallen to discover that his name was not on the guest list. This disappointment seems to have been the cause of his decision, in the summer of 1839, to invite a huge swathe of the British aristocracy to participate in a medieval tournament on his estate in Ayrshire. Rehearsals were held in St John's Wood, as Montgomerie made preparations north of the border. He constructed a Gothic pavilion to seat the guests, engaged an actor to play the part of a jester, and choreographed a mass of phoney halberdiers, servitors and men-at-arms. The whole affair owed much more to the novels of Sir Walter Scott than any archaeological actuality, but that didn't seem to bother anyone. The Earl clambered into his brass suit of armour, and held court for three days as dozens of British noblemen knocked each other off horses in the pouring rain.

Although considered by many to be a preposterous washout, the Eglinton Tournament did have its admirers. Victoria and Albert, for two. Three years later, in an attempt to aid the beleaguered British cotton-manufacturing industry, they decided to throw a medieval costume ball at Buckingham Palace. Over two thousand guests dressed up in Plantagenet gear, which had been specially woven for the occasion by British firms. The royal couple appeared in the guise of their Saxon forebears, Edward III and Queen Philippa of Hainault. Sir Edward Landseer painted their

vii

portrait, reproducing the faux-medieval robes and clasps and cloaks in exquisite detail. The gig was a PR catastrophe: instead of drumming up support for an ailing industry, Victoria and Albert were attacked in the press for their indulgence. There was, however, a more long-term positive result for British manufacturing: an aesthetic that alluded to the Middle Ages became increasingly fashionable. Furniture-makers started turning out chairs and tables that might have graced the halls of – as the opening line of Sir Walter Scott's *Ivanhoe* (1819) has it – 'that pleasant district of merry England which is watered by the river Don.' By 1851, it was possible to heat your home with stove units built to look like suits of twelfth-century armour.

All of which may help to explain what kind of book *Rebecca and Rowena* is. Here are a few more suggestions. It's a parodic sequel to *Ivanhoe*, one of the nineteenth century's most revered works of fiction. It's a Christmas panto in print. It's a debunking of the historical novel, which suggests that all such enterprises are doomed to collapse into Whiggish absurdity. It's an extremely sharp satire on the British love affair with a medieval world that never existed. It's the nearest Victorian Britain ever got to *Monty Python and the Holy Grail*.

In Thackeray's version of the twelfth century, feudal knights fly the Union Jack, puff on cigars, sip tea, consume muffins and pore over a newspaper called the *St James's Chronykyll*. A disguised Ivanhoe flits about the country in a wig and spectacles. Richard I strums his guitar and warbles his latest composition, 'Rule, Britannia!'. ('Ivanhoe,' says Thackeray, 'thought he had heard something very like the air and the words elsewhere.') This is not a novella for anachrophobes. But it is a novella for anyone who's read a book and had doubts about the happiness of its happy ending.

For many readers, *Ivanhoe* is such a book. Scott's novel tells how, in the aftermath of the Third Crusade, King Richard I and Robin Hood combine forces to wrest the throne of England back from wicked Prince John. It relates how Sir Wilfred of Ivanhoe (Wilfrid in *Rebecca and Rowena*) reclaims his lost inheritance and gains the hand of his first love, the virtuous Lady Rowena. It also describes his relationship with a rather more interesting woman – Rebecca, the daughter of a Jewish merchant named Isaac of York. Ivanhoe defends Rebecca from a charge of witchcraft, and the dubious attentions of a Templar Knight named Brian de Bois-Guilbert. Scott's quiet disposal of his heroine at the end of the book (she's packed off to Spain with her father, as Rowena gets hitched to the hero) did not prevent her from becoming the focus of his readers' attention. Indeed, William Moncrieff's 1820 stage adaptation of the book dispensed with Ivanhoe altogether, and retitled the story *The Jewess*. Thackeray makes plain his own preference: 'It ever seemed to me that Rebecca would have had the husband, and Rowena would have gone off to a convent and shut herself up where I, for one, would never have taken the trouble of enquiring for her.' In his sequel, Rowena is a grotesque hypocrite, a fervent chapelgoer who's happy to flog her servants; a tyrant who would cheerfully see all British Jews exterminated (and that's the word Thackeray uses), so jealous is she of her husband's attraction to Rebecca.

Did Thackeray's satire succeed in undermining the

fashion for medieval pastiche? Not remotely. As is evidenced by the subsequent work of Tennyson, Morris, Ruskin, Burne-Jones, and all those architects who built the neo-Gothic suburbs of our cities, it became one of the key aesthetic styles of the nineteenth century. Pugin designed a medieval court for Prince Albert's Great Exhibition. Images of the Queen and her Consort in medieval dress were sold as souvenir engravings. Their tomb at Windsor contains the couple's sculpted figures, draped in cloaks and tabards. Victoria's coronation might have been a penny-pinching affair, but her death and burial were accompanied with all the chivalric ceremony that her state could muster.

Thackeray's failure, however, has ensured that the gags in *Rebecca and Rowena* remain in good working order. Like Vikings with horned helmets and Welsh druids in white robes, the Middle Ages of the popular imagination is the product of nineteenth-century myth-making: as much a fantasy as today's fur bikini-and-scimitar school of feudal fiction. Knights in shining armour, damsels in distress, a lost England united by codes of courtly honour: these remain curiously attractive concepts. Which is why the loud and disrespectful raspberry blown by this novella remains resonant.

– Matthew Sweet, 2002

Rebecca and Rowena

CHAPTER I

The overture – commencement of the business

Well-beloved novel readers and gentle patronesses of romance, assuredly it has often occurred to every one of you that the books we delight in have very unsatisfactory conclusions, and end quite prematurely with page 320 of the third volume. At that epoch of the history it is well-known that the hero is seldom more than thirty years old, and the heroine by consequence some seven or eight years younger; and I would ask any of you whether it is fair to suppose that people after the above age have nothing worthy of note in their lives, and cease to exist as they drive away from St George's, Hanover Square? You, dear young ladies, who get your knowledge of life from the circulating library, may be led to imagine that when the marriage business is done – and Emilia is whisked off in the new travelling carriage, by the side of the enraptured Earl, or Belinda, breaking away from the tearful embraces of her excellent mother, dries her own lovely eyes upon the throbbing waistcoat of her bridegroom – you may be apt, I say, to suppose that all is over then; that Emilia and the Earl are going to be happy for the rest of their lives in his lordship's romantic castle in the north, and Belinda and her young clergyman to enjoy uninterrupted bliss in their rose-trellised parsonage in the west of England: but some there be among the novel-reading classes – old experienced folks – who know better than this. Some there be who have been married, and found that they have still something to see and to do, and to suffer mayhap; and that adventures, and pains, and pleasures, and taxes, and sunrises, and settings, and the business and joys and griefs of life go on after as before the nuptial ceremony.

Therefore, I say it is an unfair advantage, which the novelist takes of hero and heroine, as of his inexperienced reader, to say goodbye to the two former as soon as ever they are made husband and wife; and have often wished that additions should be made to all works of fiction which have been brought to abrupt terminations in the manner described; and that we should hear what occurs to the sober married man as well as to the ardent bachelor, to the matron as well as to the blushing spinster. And in this respect I admire (and would desire to imitate) the noble and prolific French author, Alexandre Dumas, Marquis Davy de la Pailleterie, who carries his heroes from early youth down to the most venerable old age, and does not let them rest until they are so old that it is full time the poor fellows should get a little peace and quiet. A hero is much too valuable a gentleman to be put upon the retired list in the prime and vigour of his youth, and I wish to know what lady among us would like to be put on the shelf, and thought no longer interesting, because she has a family growing up and is four or five and thirty years of age? I have known ladies at sixty with hearts as tender, and ideas as romantic, as any young misses of sixteen. Let us have middle-aged novels, then, as well as your extremely juvenile legends. Let the young ones be warned that the old folks have a right to be interesting, and that a lady may continue to have a heart although she is somewhat stouter than she was when a schoolgirl, and a man his feelings although he gets his hair from Truefitt's.

This I would desire: that the biographies of many of our most illustrious personages of romance should be continued by fitting hands, and that they should be heard of until at least a decent age. Look at Mr James' heroes: they invariably marry young. Look at Mr Dickens': they disappear from the scene when they are mere chits. I trust these authors, who are still alive, will see the propriety of telling us something more about people in whom we took a considerable interest, and who must be at present strong and hearty, and in the full vigour of health and intellect. And in the tales of the great Sir Walter (may honour be to his name), I am sure there are a number of people who are untimely carried away from us, and of whom we ought to hear more.

My dear Rebecca, daughter of Isaac of York, has always, in my mind, been one of these. Nor can I ever believe that such a woman, so admirable, so tender, so heroic, so beautiful, could disappear altogether before such another woman as Rowena, that vapid, flaxen-haired creature who is, in my humble opinion, unworthy of Ivanhoe, and unworthy of her place as a heroine. Had both of them got their rights, it ever seemed to me that Rebecca would have had the husband, and Rowena would have gone off to a convent and shut herself up, where I, for one, would never have taken the trouble of enquiring for her.

But after all she married Ivanhoe. What is to be done? There is no help for it. There it is in black and white, at the end of the third volume of Sir Walter Scott's chronicle, that the couple were joined together in matrimony. And must the disinherited knight, whose blood has been warmed in the company of the tender and beautiful Rebecca, sit down contented for life by the side of such a frigid piece of propriety as that icy, faultless, prim, niminy-piminy Rowena? Forbid it Fate, forbid it poetical justice! There is a simple plan for setting matters right, and giving all parties their due, which is here submitted to the novel reader. Ivanhoe's history *must* have had a continuation, and it is this which ensues. I may be wrong in some particulars of the narrative – as what writer will not be? – but of the main incidents of the history I have in my own mind no sort of doubt, and confidently submit them to that generous public which likes to see virtue righted, true love rewarded, and the brilliant fairy descend out of the blazing chariot at the end of the pantomime, and make Harlequin and Columbine happy. What if reality be not so, gentlemen and ladies, and if, after dancing a variety of jigs and antics, and jumping in and out of endless trapdoors and windows, through life's shifting scenes, no fairy comes down to make *us* comfortable at the close of the performance? Ah! let us give our honest novel-folks the benefit of their position, and not be envious of their good luck.

No person who has read the preceding volumes of this history, as the famous chronicler of Abbotsford has recorded them, can doubt for a moment what was the result of the marriage between Sir Wilfrid of Ivanhoe and the Lady Rowena. Those who have marked her conduct during her maidenhood, her distinguished politeness, her spotless modesty of demeanour, her unalterable coolness under all circumstances, and her lofty and gentlewoman-like bearing, must be sure that her married conduct would equal her spinster behaviour, and that Rowena the wife would be a pattern of correctness for all the matrons of England.

6

Such was the fact. For miles around Rotherwood her character for piety was known. Her castle was a rendezvous for all the clergy and monks of the district, whom she fed with the richest viands, while she pinched herself upon pulse and water. There was not an invalid in the three Ridings, Saxon or Norman, but the palfrey of the Lady Rowena might be seen journeying to his door in company with Father Glauber, her almoner, and Brother Thomas of Epsom, her leech. She lit up all the churches in Yorkshire with wax candles, the offerings of her piety. The bells of her chapel began to ring at two o'clock in the morning, and all the domestics of Rotherwood were called upon to attend at matins, at complines, at nones, at vespers, and at sermon. I need not say that fasting was observed with all the rigours of the Church, and that those of the servants of the Lady Rowena were looked upon with most favour whose hair shirts were the roughest, and who flagellated themselves with the most becoming perseverance.

Whether it was that this discipline cleared poor Wamba's wits or cooled his humour, it is certain that he became the most melancholy fool in England, and if ever he ventured upon a pun to the shuddering, poor servitors, who were mumbling their dry crusts below the salt, it was such a faint and stale joke that nobody dared to laugh at the innuendoes of the unfortunate wag, and a sickly smile was the best applause he could muster. Once, indeed, when Guffo, the goose-boy (a half-witted, poor wretch), laughed outright at a lamentably stale pun which Wamba palmed upon him at supper-time (it was dark, and the torches being brought in, Wamba said, 'Guffo, they can't see their way in the argument, and are going *to throw a little light on the subject*'), the Lady Rowena, being disturbed in a theological controversy with Father Willibald (afterwards canonised as St Willibald of Bareacres, hermit and confessor), called out to know what was the cause of the unseemly interruption, and Guffo and Wamba being pointed out as the culprits, ordered them straight away into the courtyard, and three dozen to be administered to each of them.

'I got you out of Front-de-Boeuf's castle,' said poor Wamba, piteously, appealing to Sir Wilfrid of Ivanhoe, 'and canst thou not save me from the lash?'

'Yes, from Front-de-Boeuf's castle, *where you were locked up with the Jewess in the tower!*' said Rowena, haughtily replying to the timid appeal of her husband. 'Gurth, give him four dozen!'

And this was all poor Wamba got by applying for the mediation of his master.

In fact, Rowena knew her own dignity so well as a princess of the royal blood of England that Sir Wilfrid of Ivanhoe, her consort, could scarcely call his life his own, and was made in all things to feel the inferiority of his station. And which of us is there acquainted with the sex that has not remarked this propensity in lovely woman, and how often the wisest in the council are made to be as fools at *her* board, and the boldest in the battlefield are craven when facing *her* distaff?

'*Where you were locked up with the Jewess in the tower,*' was a remark, too, of which Wilfrid keenly felt, and perhaps the reader will understand the significance. When the daughter of Isaac of York brought her diamonds and rubies – the poor, gentle victim! – and, meekly laying them at the feet of the conquering Rowena, departed into foreign lands to tend the sick of her people, and to brood over the bootless passion which consumed her own pure heart, one would have thought that the heart of the royal lady would have melted before such beauty and humility, and that she would have been generous in the moment of her victory.

But did you ever know a right-minded woman pardon another for being handsome and more love-worthy than herself? The Lady Rowena did certainly say with mighty magnanimity to the Jewish maiden, 'Come and live with me as a sister', as the former part of this history shows, but Rebecca knew in her heart that her ladyship's proposition was what is called '*bosh*' (in that noble Eastern language with which Wilfrid the Crusader was familiar), or 'fudge' in plain Saxon, and retired with a broken, gentle spirit, neither able to bear the sight of her rival's happiness nor willing to disturb it by the contrast of her own wretchedness. Rowena, like the most high-bred and virtuous of women, never forgave Isaac's daughter her beauty nor her flirtation with Wilfrid (as the Saxon lady chose to term it), nor, above all, her admirable diamonds and jewels, although Rowena was actually in possession of them.

In a word, she was always flinging Rebecca into Ivanhoe's teeth. There was not a day in his life but that unhappy warrior was made to remember that a Hebrew damsel had been in love with him, and that a Christian lady of fashion could never forgive the insult. For instance, if Gurth, the swineherd, who was now promoted to be gamekeeper and verderer, brought the account of a famous wild boar of the wood and proposed a hunt, Rowena would say, 'Do, Sir Wilfrid, persecute those poor pigs – you know your friends the Jews can't abide them!' Or when, as it oft

9

would happen, our lion-hearted monarch, Richard, in order to get a loan or a benevolence from the Jews, would roast a few of the Hebrew capitalists, or extract some of the principal rabbis' teeth, Rowena would exult and say, 'Serve them right, the misbelieving wretches! England can never be a happy country until every one of these monsters is exterminated!' Or else, adopting a strain of still more savage sarcasm, would exclaim, 'Ivanhoe, my dear, more persecution for the Jews! Hadn't you better interfere, my love? His Majesty will do anything for you, and, you know, the Jews were *always such favourites of yours*,' or words to that effect. But, nevertheless, her ladyship never lost an opportunity of wearing Rebecca's jewels at court, whenever the Queen held a drawing-room, or at the York assizes and ball, when she appeared there, not of course because she took any interest in such things, but because she considered it her duty to attend as one of the chief ladies of the county.

Thus Sir Wilfrid of Ivanhoe, having attained the height of his wishes, was, like many a man when he has reached that dangerous elevation, disappointed. Ah, dear friends, it is but too often so in life! Many a garden, seen from a distance, looks fresh and green, which, when beheld closely, is dismal and weedy: the shady walks melancholy and grass-grown, the bowers you would fain repose in, cushioned with stinging nettles. I have ridden in a caique upon the waters of the Bosporus, and looked upon the capital of the Soldan of Turkey. As seen from those blue waters, with palace and pinnacle, with gilded dome and towering cypress, it seemeth a very Paradise of Mahound, but enter the city, and it is but a beggarly labyrinth of rickety huts and dirty alleys, where the ways are steep and the smells are foul, tenanted by mangy dogs and ragged beggars – a dismal illusion! Life is such, ah, well-a-day! It is only hope which is real, and reality is a bitterness and a deceit.

Perhaps a man with Ivanhoe's high principles would never bring himself to acknowledge this fact, but others did for him. He grew thin, and pined away as much as if he had been in a fever under the scorching sun of Ascalon. He had no appetite for his meals, he slept ill, though he was yawning all day. The jangling of the doctors and friars whom Rowena brought together did not in the least enliven him, and he would sometimes give proofs of somnolency during their disputes, greatly to the consternation of his lady. He hunted a good deal and, I very much fear, as Rowena rightly remarked, that he might have an excuse for being absent from home. He began to like wine, too, who had been as sober as a hermit, and when he came back from Athelstane's (whither he would repair not infrequently), the unsteadiness of his gait and the unnatural brilliancy of his eye were remarked by his lady, who, you may be sure, was sitting up for him. As for Athelstane, he swore by St Wullstan that he was glad to have escaped a marriage with such a pattern of propriety, and honest Cedric the Saxon (who had been very speedily driven out of his daughter-in-law's castle) vowed by St Waltheof that his son had bought a dear bargain.

So Sir Wilfrid of Ivanhoe became almost as tired of England as his royal master Richard was (who always quitted the country when he had squeezed from his loyal nobles, commons, clergy, and Jews all the money which he could get), and when the lion-hearted prince began to make war against the French king, in Normandy and Guienne,

Sir Wilfrid pined like a true servant to be in company of the good champion, alongside of whom he had shivered so many lances, and dealt such woundy blows of sword and battleaxe on the plains of Jaffa, or the breaches of Acre. Travellers were welcome at Rotherwood that brought news of the camp of the good king, and I warrant me that the knight listened with all his might when Father Drono, the chaplain, read in *St James's Chronykyll* (which was the paper of news he of Ivanhoe took in) of 'another glorious triumph' – 'Defeat of the French near Blois'; 'Splendid victory at Epte, and narrow escape of the French king' – the which deeds of arms the learned scribes had to narrate.

However such tales might excite him during the reading, they left the Knight of Ivanhoe only the more melancholy after listening, and the more moody as he sate in his great hall silently draining his Gascony wine. Silently sat he and looked at his coats of mail hanging vacant on the wall, his banner covered with spider webs and his sword and axe rusting there. 'Ah, dear axe,' sighed he (into his drinking-horn) – 'ah, gentle steel! That was a merry time when I sent thee crashing into the pate of the Emir Abdul Melik as he rode on the right of Saladin. Ah, my sword, my dainty headsman, my sweet split-rib, my razor of infidel beards, is the rust to eat thine edge off, and am I never more to wield thee in battle? What is the use of a shield on a wall, or a lance that has a cobweb for a pennon? O, Richard, my good king, would I could hear once more thy voice in the front of the onset! Bones of Brian the Templar, would ye could rise from your grave at Templestowe, and that we might break another spear for honour and – and –'

'And *Rebecca*,' he would have said – but the knight

paused here in rather a guilty panic, and her Royal Highness the Princess Rowena (as she chose to style herself at home) looked so hard at him out of her china-blue eyes that Sir Wilfrid felt as if she was reading his thoughts, and was fain to drop his own eyes into his flagon.

In a word, his life was intolerable. The dinner hour of the twelfth century, it is known, was very early: in fact people dined at ten o'clock in the morning. And after dinner Rowena sat mum under her canopy, embroidered with the arms of Edward the Confessor, working with her maidens at the most hideous pieces of tapestry, representing the tortures and the martyrdoms of her favourite saints, and not allowing a soul to speak above his breath, except when she chose to cry out in her own shrill voice when a handmaid made a wrong stitch, or let fall a ball of worsted. It was a dreary life. Wamba, we have said, never ventured to crack a joke, save in a whisper, when he was ten miles from home; and then Sir Wilfrid Ivanhoe was too weary and blue-devilled to laugh, but hunted in silence, moodily bringing down deer and wild boar with shaft and quarrel.

Then he besought Robin of Huntingdon, the jolly outlaw, nonetheless, to join him, and go to the help of the fair sire King Richard, with a score or two of lances. But the Earl of Huntingdon was a very different character from Robin Hood the forester. There was no more conscientious magistrate in all the county than his lordship. He was never known to miss church or quarter sessions. He was the strictest game proprietor in all the riding, and sent scores of poachers to Botany Bay. 'A man who has a stake in the country, my good Sir Wilfrid,' Lord Huntingdon said, with rather a patronising air (his lordship had grown immensely fat since the King had taken him into grace, and required a horse as strong as an elephant to mount him), 'a man with a stake in the country ought to stay *in* the country. Property has its duties as well as its privileges, and a person of my rank is bound to live on the land from which he gets his living.'

'Amen!' sang out the Reverend Tuck, his lordship's domestic chaplain, who had also grown as sleek as the Abbot of Jorvaulx, who was as prim as a lady in his dress, wore bergamot in his handkerchief, and had his poll shaved and his beard curled every day. And so sanctified was his Reverence grown that he thought it was a shame to kill the pretty deer (though he ate of them still hugely, both in pasties and with French beans and currant jelly), and being shown a quarterstaff upon a certain occasion, handled it curiously and asked what that ugly great stick was.

Lady Huntingdon, late Maid Marian, had still some of her own fun and spirits, and poor Ivanhoe begged and prayed that she would come and stay at Rotherwood occasionally, and *égayer* the general dullness of that castle. But her ladyship said that Rowena gave herself such airs, and bored her so intolerably with stories of King Edward the Confessor, that she preferred any place rather than Rotherwood, which was as dull as if it had been at the top of Mount Athos.

The only person who visited it was Athelstane. 'His Royal Highness the Prince', Rowena of course called him, whom the lady received with royal honours. She had the guns fired, and the footmen turned out with presented arms when he arrived, helped him to all Ivanhoe's favourite cuts of the mutton or the turkey, and forced her poor husband to light him to the state bedroom, walking backwards, holding a pair of wax candles. At this hour of bedtime the thane used to be in such a condition that he saw two pair of candles and a couple of Ivanhoes reeling before him – let us hope it was not Ivanhoe that was reeling, but only his kinsman's brains muddled with the quantities of drink which it was his daily custom to consume. Rowena said it was the crack which the wicked Bois-Guilbert, 'the Jewess' *other* lover, Wilfrid, my dear,' gave him on his royal skull, which caused the Prince to be disturbed so easily, but added that drinking became a person of royal blood, and was but one of the duties of his station.

Sir Wilfrid of Ivanhoe saw it would be of no avail to ask this man to bear him company on his projected tour abroad, but still he himself was every day more and more bent upon going, and he long cast about for some means of breaking to his Rowena his firm resolution to join the King. He thought she would certainly fall ill if he communicated the news too abruptly to her. He would pretend a journey to York to attend a grand jury; then a call to London on a law business or to buy stock; then he would slip over to Calais by the packet by degrees, as it were; and so be with the King before his wife knew that he was out of sight of Westminster Hall.

'Suppose your honour says you are going, as your honour would say boo to a goose, plump, short, and to the point,' said Wamba the jester, who was Sir Wilfrid's chief counsellor and attendant, 'depend on it, Her Highness would bear the news like a Christian woman.'

'Tush, malapert! I will give thee the strap,' said Sir Wilfrid, in a fine tone of high-tragedy indignation. 'Thou knowest not the delicacy of the nerves of high-born ladies. An she faint not, write me down Hollander.'

'I will wager my bauble against an Irish billet of exchange that she will let your honour go off readily: that is, if you press not the matter too strongly,' Wamba answered, knowingly. And this Ivanhoe found to his discomfiture: for one morning at breakfast, adopting a *dégagé* air, as he sipped his tea, he said, 'My love, I was thinking of going over to pay His Majesty a visit in Normandy.' Upon which, laying down her muffin (which, since the royal Alfred baked those cakes, had been the chosen breakfast cate of noble Anglo-Saxons, and which a kneeling page tendered to her on a salver, chased by the Florentine Benvenuto Cellini) – 'When do you think of going, Wilfrid, my dear?' the lady said, and the moment the tea-things were removed, and the tables and their trestles put away, she set about mending his linen, and getting ready his carpet-bag.

So Sir Wilfrid was as disgusted at her readiness to part with him as he had been weary of staying at home, which caused Wamba the fool to say, 'Marry, gossip, thou art like the man on shipboard, who, when the boatswain flogged him, did cry out "Oh!" wherever the rope's end fell on him: which caused Master Boatswain to say, "Plague on thee, fellow, and a pox on thee, knave, wherever I hit thee there is no pleasing thee."'

'And truly there are some backs which Fortune is always belabouring,' thought Sir Wilfrid with a groan, 'and mine is one that is ever sore.'

So, with a moderate retinue, whereof the knave Wamba made one, and a large woollen comforter round his neck, which his wife's own white fingers had woven, Sir Wilfrid of Ivanhoe left home to join the King, his master. Rowena, standing on the steps, poured out a series of long prayers and blessings, most edifying to hear, as her lord mounted his charger, which his squires led to the door. 'It was the duty of the British female of rank,' she said, 'to suffer all, *all* in the cause of her Sovereign. *She* would not fear loneliness during the campaign: she would bear up against widowhood, desertion, and an unprotected situation.'

'My cousin Athelstane will protect thee,' said Ivanhoe, with profound emotion, as the tears trickled down his basinet; and bestowing a chaste salute upon the steel-clad warrior, Rowena modestly said she hoped His Highness would be so kind.

Then Ivanhoe's trumpet blew. Then Rowena waved her pocket-handkerchief. Then the household gave a shout. Then the pursuivant of the good knight, Sir Wilfrid the Crusader, flung out his banner (which was argent, a gules cramoisy with three Moors impaled sable). Then Wamba gave a lash on his mule's haunch, and Ivanhoe, heaving a great sigh, turned the tail of his warhorse upon the castle of his fathers.

As they rode along the forest they met Athelstane, the thane, powdering along the road in the direction of Rotherwood on his great dray-horse of a charger. 'Goodbye, good luck to you, old brick,' cried the Prince, using the vernacular Saxon. 'Pitch into those Frenchmen, give it 'em over the face and eyes, and I'll stop at home and take care of Mrs I.'

'Thank you, kinsman,' said Ivanhoe, looking, however, not particularly well pleased; and the chiefs shaking hands, the train of each took its different way – Athelstane's to

Rotherwood, Ivanhoe's towards his place of embarkation.

The poor knight had his wish, and yet his face was a yard long, and as yellow as a lawyer's parchment; and having longed to quit home any time these three years past, he found himself envying Athelstane, because, forsooth, he was going to Rotherwood: which symptoms of discontent being observed by the witless Wamba, caused that absurd madman to bring his rebec over his shoulder from his back, and to sing:

Atra cura

Before I lost my five poor wits,
I mind me of a Romish clerk,
Who sang how Care, the phantom dark,
Beside the belted horseman sits.
Methought I saw the grisly sprite
Jump up but now behind my Knight.

'Perhaps thou didst, knave,' said Ivanhoe, looking over his shoulder, and the knave went on with his jingle.

And though he gallop as he may,
I mark that cursed monster black
Still sits behind his honour's back,
Tight squeezing of his heart alway.
Like two black Templars sit they there,
Beside one crupper, Knight and Care.

No knight am I with pennoned spear,
To prance upon a bold destrere:

I will not have black Care prevail
Upon my long-eared charger's tail,
For lo, I am a witless fool,
And laugh at grief and ride a mule.

And his bells rattled as he kicked his mule's sides.

'Silence, fool!' said Sir Wilfrid of Ivanhoe, in a voice both majestic and wrathful. 'If thou knowest not care and grief, it is because thou knowest not love, whereof they are the companions. Who can love without an anxious heart? How shall there be joy at meeting, without tears at parting?' (I did not see that his honour or my lady shed many anon, thought Wamba the fool; but he was only a zany, and his mind was not right.) 'I would not exchange my very sorrows for thine indifference,' the knight continued. 'Where there is a sun there must be a shadow. If the shadow offend me, shall I put out my eyes and live in the dark? No! I am content with my fate, even such as it is. The Care of which thou speakest, hard though it may vex him, never yet rode down an honest man. I can bear him on my shoulders, and make my way through the world's press in spite of him, for my arm is strong, and my sword is keen, and my shield has no stain on it; and my heart, though it is sad, knows no guile.' And here, taking a locket out of his waistcoat (which was made out of chain-mail), the knight kissed the token, put it back under the waistcoat again, heaved a profound sigh, and stuck spurs into his horse.

As for Wamba, he was munching a black pudding whilst Sir Wilfrid was making the above speech (which implied some secret grief on the knight's part that must have been perfectly unintelligible to the fool), and so did not listen to a single word of Ivanhoe's pompous remarks. They travelled on by slow stages through the whole kingdom, until they came to Dover, whence they took shipping for Calais. And in this little voyage, being exceedingly seasick, and besides elated at the thought of meeting his Sovereign, the good knight cast away that profound melancholy which had accompanied him during the whole of his land journey.

CHAPTER II

The last days of the Lion

From Calais Sir Wilfrid of Ivanhoe took the diligence across country to Limoges, sending on Gurth, his squire, with the horses and the rest of his attendants, with the exception of Wamba, who travelled not only as the knight's fool but as his valet, and who, perched on the roof of the carriage, amused himself by blowing tunes upon the *conducteur's* French horn. The good King Richard was, as Ivanhoe learned, in the Limousin, encamped before a little place called Chalus; the lord whereof, though a vassal of the King's, was holding the castle against his Sovereign with a resolution and valour which caused a great fury and annoyance on the part of the monarch with the lion-heart. For, brave and magnanimous as he was, the Lion-hearted one did not love to be baulked any more than another; and, like the royal animal whom he was said to resemble, he commonly tore his adversary to pieces, and then, per-chance, had leisure to think how brave the latter had been. The Count of Chalus had found, it was said, a pot of money: the royal Richard wanted it. As the count denied that he had it, why did he not open the gates of his town at once? It was a clear proof that he was guilty, and the King was determined to punish this rebel, and have his money and his life too.

He had naturally brought no breaching guns with him, because those instruments were not yet invented, and though he had assaulted the place a score of times with the utmost fury, His Majesty had been beaten back on every

21

occasion, until he was so savage that it was dangerous to approach the British Lion. The Lion's wife, the lovely Berengaria, scarcely ventured to come near him. He flung the joint-stools in his tent at the heads of the Officers of State, and kicked his aides-de-camp round his pavilion; and, in fact, a maid of honour, who brought a sack-posset unto His Majesty from the Queen after he came in from the assault, came spinning like a football out of the royal tent just as Ivanhoe entered it.

'Send me my Austrian drum-major to flog that woman,' roared out the infuriate King. 'By the bones of St Barnabas, she has burned the sack! By St Wittikind, I will have her flayed alive. Ha, St George! ha St Richard! whom have we here?' And he lifted up the demi-culverin, or curtal-axe, a weapon weighing about thirteen hundredweight, and was about to fling it at the intruder's head, when the latter, kneeling gracefully on one knee, said calmly, 'It is I, my good liege, Wilfrid of Ivanhoe.'

'What, Wilfrid of Templestowe, Wilfrid the married man, Wilfrid the henpecked!' cried the King with a sudden burst of good humour, flinging away the culverin from him as though it had been a reed (it lighted three hundred yards off, on the foot of Hugo de Bunyon, who was smoking a cigar at the foot of his tent, and caused that redoubted warrior to limp for some days after). 'What, Wilfrid, my gossip? Art come to see the Lion's den? There are bones in it, man, bones and carcasses, and the Lion is angry,' said the King, with a terrific glare of his eyes. 'But tush! we will talk of that anon. Ho! bring two gallons of hypocras for the King and the good knight, Wilfrid of Ivanhoe. Thou art come in time, Wilfrid, for by St Richard and St George, we will give a grand assault tomorrow. There will be bones broken, ha!'

'I care not my liege,' said Ivanhoe, pledging the Sovereign respectfully, and tossing off the whole contents of the bowl of hypocras to His Highness' good health – and he at once appeared to be thus taken into high favour, not a little to the envy of many of the persons surrounding the King.

As His Majesty said, there was fighting and feasting in plenty before Chalus. Day after day the besiegers made assaults upon the castle, but it was held so stoutly by the Count of Chalus and his gallant garrison that each afternoon beheld the attacking parties returning disconsolately to their tents, leaving behind them many of their own slain, and bringing back with them store of broken heads and maimed limbs, received in the unsuccessful onset. The valour displayed by Ivanhoe in all these contests was prodigious; and the way in which he escaped death from the discharges of mangonels, catapults, battering-rams, twenty-four pounders, boiling oil, and other artillery with which the besieged received their enemies, was remarkable. After a day's fighting, Gurth and Wamba used to pick the arrows out of their intrepid master's coat of mail as if they had been so many almonds in a pudding. It was well for the good knight that under his first coat of armour he wore a choice suit of Toledan steel, perfectly impervious to arrow shots, and given to him by a certain Jew named Isaac of York, to whom he had done some considerable services a few years back.

If King Richard had not been in such a rage at the repeated failures of his attacks upon the castle that all sense of justice was blinded in the lion-hearted monarch, he would have been the first to acknowledge the valour of Sir Wilfrid of Ivanhoe, and would have given him a peerage and the Grand Cross of the Bath at least a dozen times in the course of the siege. For Ivanhoe led more than a dozen storming parties, and with his own hand killed as many men (viz. two thousand three hundred and fifty-one, within six) as were slain by the lion-hearted monarch himself. But His Majesty was rather disgusted than pleased by his faithful servant's prowess, and all the courtiers, who hated Ivanhoe for his superior valour and dexterity (for he would kill you off a couple of hundred of them of Chalus, whilst the strongest champions of the King's host could not finish more than their two dozen of a day), poisoned the royal mind against Sir Wilfrid, and made the King look upon his feats of arms with an evil eye. Roger de Backbite sneeringly told the King that Sir Wilfrid had offered to bet an equal bet that he would kill more men than Richard himself in the next assault. Peter de Toadhole said that Ivanhoe stated everywhere that His Majesty was not the man he used to be; that pleasures and drink had enervated him; that he could neither ride nor strike a blow with sword or axe as he had been enabled to do in the old times in Palestine. And finally, in the twenty-fifth assault, in which they had very nearly carried the place, and in which onset Ivanhoe slew seven, and His Majesty six of the sons of the Count de Chalus, its defender, Ivanhoe almost did for himself, by planting his banner before the King's upon the wall; and only rescued himself from utter disgrace by saving His Majesty's life several times in the course of this most desperate onslaught.

Then the luckless knight's very virtues (as, no doubt, my respected readers know) made him enemies amongst the men – nor was Ivanhoe liked by the women frequenting the camp of the gay King Richard. His young Queen and a brilliant court of ladies attended the pleasure-loving monarch. His Majesty would transact business in the morning, then fight severely from after breakfast till about three o'clock in the afternoon, from which time until after midnight there was nothing but jigging and singing, feasting and revelry in the royal tents. Ivanhoe, who was asked as a master of ceremony and forced to attend these entertainments, not caring about the blandishments of any of the ladies present, looked on at their ogling and dancing with a countenance as glum as an undertaker's, and was a perfect wet blanket in the midst of the festivities. His favourite resort and conversation were with a remarkably austere hermit who lived in the neighbourhood of Chalus, and with whom Ivanhoe loved to talk about Palestine and the Jews, and other grave matters of import, better than to mingle in the gayest amusements of the Court of King Richard. Many a night, when the Queen and the ladies were dancing quadrilles and polkas (in which His Majesty, who was enormously stout as well as tall, insisted upon figuring, and in which he was about as graceful as an elephant dancing a hornpipe), Ivanhoe would steal away from the ball, and come and have a night's chat under the moon with his reverend friend. It pained him to see a man of the King's age and size dancing about with the young folks. They laughed at His Majesty whilst they flattered him: the pages and maids of honour mimicked the royal mountebank almost to his face; and, if Ivanhoe ever could have laughed, he certainly would have one night, when the King, in light-blue satin inexpressibles, with his hair in powder, chose to dance the Minuet de la Cour with the little Queen Berengaria.

Then, after dancing, His Majesty must needs order a

guitar and begin to sing. He was said to compose his own songs – words and music – but those who have read Lord Campobello's *Lives of the Lord Chancellors* are aware that there was a person by the name of Blondel who, in fact, did all the musical part of the King's performances; and, as for the words, when a king writes verses we may be sure there will be plenty of people to admire his poetry. His Majesty would sing you a ballad, of which he had stolen every idea, to an air which was ringing on all the barrel-organs of Christendom, and, turning round to his courtiers, would say, 'How do you like that? I dashed it off this morning.' Or, 'Blondel, what do you think of this movement in B flat?' or whatnot. And the courtiers and Blondel, you may be sure, would applaud with all their might, like hypocrites as they were.

One evening – it was the evening of the 27th March 1199, indeed – His Majesty, who was in the musical mood, treated the Court with a quantity of his so-called compositions, until the people were fairly tired of clapping with their hands and laughing in their sleeves. First he sang an *original* air and poem, beginning:

> *Cherries nice, cherries nice, nice, come choose*
> *Fresh and fair ones, who'll refuse? etc.*

The which he was ready to take his affidavit he had composed the day before yesterday. Then he sang an *original* heroic melody, of which the chorus was:

> *Rule Britannia, Britannia rules the sea,*
> *For Britons never, never, never slaves shall be, etc.*

The courtiers applauded this song as they did the other – all except Ivanhoe, who sat without changing a muscle of his features – until the King questioned him, when the knight with a bow said he thought he had heard something very like the air and the words elsewhere. His Majesty scowled at him a savage glance from under his red bushy eyebrows, but Ivanhoe had saved the royal life that day, and the King therefore with difficulty controlled his indignation.

'Well,' said he, 'by St Richard and St George, but ye never heard *this* song, for I composed it this very afternoon as I took my bath after the mêlée. Did I not, Blondel?'

Blondel, of course, was ready to take an affidavit that His Majesty had done as he said, and the King, thrumming on his guitar with his great red fingers and thumbs, began to sing out of tune, and as follows:

Commanders of the faithful

The Pope he is a happy man,
His palace is the Vatican:
And there he sits and drains his can,
The Pope he is a happy man.
I often say when I'm at home,
I'd like to be the Pope of Rome.

And then there's Sultan Saladin,
That Turkish Soldan full of sin;
He has a hundred wives at least
By which his pleasure is increased;
I've often wished, I hope no sin,
That I were Sultan Saladin.

But no, the Pope no wife may choose,
   And so I would not wear his shoes;
No wine may drink the proud Paynim,
   And so I'd rather not be him;
My wife, my wine, I love I hope,
   And would be neither Turk nor Pope.

'Encore! Encore! Bravo! *Bis!*' Everybody applauded the King's song with all his might – everybody except Ivanhoe, who preserved his abominable gravity; and when asked aloud by Roger de Backbite whether he had heard that too, said firmly, 'Yes, Roger de Backbite, and so hast thou if thou darest but tell the truth.'

'Now, by St Cicely, may I never touch gittern again,' bawled the King in a fury, 'if ever note, word and thought be not mine. May I die in tomorrow's onslaught if the song be not my song. Sing thyself, Wilfrid of the Lanthorn Jaws, thou couldst sing a good song in old times.' And with all his might, and with a forced laugh, the King, who loved brutal practical jests, flung his guitar at the head of Ivanhoe.

Sir Wilfrid caught it gracefully with one hand, and, making an elegant bow to the Sovereign, began to chant as follows:

King Canute

King Canute was weary-hearted;
   he had reigned for years a score;
Battling, struggling, pushing, fighting,
   killing much and robbing more,
And he thought upon his actions,
   walking by the wild seashore.

'Twixt the Chancellor and Bishop
    walked the King with steps sedate,
Chamberlains and grooms came after,
    silver sticks and gold sticks great,
Chaplains, aides-de-camp, and pages –
    all the officers of state.

Sliding after like his shadow,
    pausing when he chose to pause;
If a frown his face contracted,
    straight the courtiers dropped their jaws;
If to laugh the King was minded,
    out they burst in loud hee-haws.

But that day a something vexed him,
    that was clear to old and young,
Thrice his Grace had yawned at table,
    when his favourite gleeman sung,
Once the Queen would have consoled him,
    but he bade her hold her tongue.

'Something ails my gracious Master,'
    cried the Keeper of the Seal,
'Sure, my lord, it is the lampreys
    served at dinner, or the veal!'
'Psha!' exclaimed the angry monarch,
    'Keeper, 'tis not that I feel.

' 'Tis the heart, and not the dinner,
    fool, that doth my rest impair;
Can a King be great as I am,

prithee, and yet know no care?
Oh, I'm sick, and tired, and weary.'
   Someone cried, 'The King's armchair!'

Then towards the lackeys turning,
   quick my lord the Keeper nodded,
Straight the King's great chair was brought him
   by two footmen able-bodied;
Languidly he sank into it;
   it was comfortably wadded.

'Leading on my fierce companions,'
   cried he, 'over storm and brine,
I have fought and I have conquered!
   Where was glory like to mine?'
Loudly all the courtiers echoed:
   'Where is glory like to thine?'

'What avail me all my kingdoms?
   Weary am I now, and old;
Those fair sons I have begotten,
   long to see me dead and cold;
Would I were, and quiet buried,
   underneath the silent mould!

'Oh, remorse, the writhing serpent!
   at my bosom tears and bites;
Horrid, horrid things I look on,
   though I put out all the lights;
Ghosts of ghastly recollections
   troop about my bed of nights.

'Cities burning, convents blazing,
    red with sacrilegious fires;
Mothers weeping, virgins screaming,
    vainly for their slaughtered sires –'
'Such a tender conscience,' cries the
    Bishop, 'every one admires.

'But for such unpleasant bygones,
    cease, my gracious Lord, to search;
They're forgotten and forgiven
    by our holy Mother Church;
Never, never does she leave her
    benefactors in the lurch.

'Look! the land is crowned with minsters,
    which your Grace's bounty raised;
Abbeys filled with holy men, where
    you and heaven are daily praised;
You, my lord, to think of dying?
    On my conscience, I'm amazed!'

'Nay, I feel,' replied King Canute,
    'that my end is drawing near.'
'Don't say so,' exclaimed the courtiers
    (striving each to squeeze a tear),
'Sure your Grace is strong and lusty,
    and may live this fifty year.'

'Live these fifty years!' the Bishop
    roared, with actions made to suit,
'Are you mad, my good Lord Keeper,

thus to speak of King Canute?
Men have lived a thousand years, and
    sure His Majesty will do't.

'Adam, Enoch, Lamech, Canan,
    Mahaleel, Methusela,
Lived nine hundred years apiece, and
    mayn't the King as well as they?'
'Fervently,' exclaimed the Keeper,
    'fervently I trust he may.'

'He to die?' resumed the Bishop.
    'He a mortal like to us?
Death was not for him intended,
    though communis omnibus;
Keeper, you are irreligious,
    for to talk and cavil thus.

'With his wondrous skill in healing
    ne'er a doctor can compete,
Loathsome lepers, if he touch them,
    start up clean upon their feet;
Surely he could raise the dead up,
    did His Highness think it meet.

'Did not once the Jewish captain
    stay the sun upon the hill,
And, the while he slew the foemen,
    bid the silver moon stand still?
So, no doubt, could gracious Canute,
    if it were his sacred will.'

'Might I stay the sun above us,
    good Sir Bishop?' Canute cried;
'Could I bid the silver moon to
    pause upon her heavenly ride?
If the moon obeys my orders,
    sure I can command the tide.

'Will the advancing waves obey me,
    Bishop, if I make the sign?'
Said the Bishop, bowing lowly,
    'Land and sea, my lord, are thine.'
Canute turned towards the ocean –
    'Back!' he said, 'thou foaming brine.

'From the sacred shore I stand on,
    I command thee to retreat;
Venture not, thou stormy rebel,
    to approach thy master's seat;
Ocean, be thou still! I bid thee
    come not nearer to my feet!'

But the sullen ocean answered
    with a louder, deeper roar,
And the rapid waves drew nearer,
    falling sounding on the shore;
Back the Keeper and the Bishop,
    back the King and courtiers bore.

And he sternly bade them never
    more to kneel to human clay,
But alone to praise and worship

That which earth and seas obey,
And his golden crown of empire
never wore he from that day.
King Canute is dead and gone:
parasites exist alway.

At this ballad, which, to be sure, was awfully long, and as grave as a sermon, some of the courtiers tittered, some yawned, and some affected to be asleep and snore outright. But Roger de Backbite, thinking to curry favour with the King by this piece of vulgarity, His Majesty fetched him a knock on the nose and a buffet on the ear, which, I warrant me, wakened Master Roger, to whom the King said, 'Listen, and be civil, slave; Wilfrid is singing about thee. Wilfrid, thy ballad is long, but it is to the purpose, and I have grown cool during thy homily. Give me thy hand, honest friend. Ladies, good night. Gentlemen, we give the grand assault tomorrow, when I promise thee, Wilfrid, thy banner shall not be before mine.' And the King, giving his arm to Her Majesty, retired into the private pavilion.

CHAPTER III

St George for England

Whilst the royal Richard and his Court were feasting in the camp outside the walls of Chalus, they of the castle were in the most miserable plight that might be conceived. Hunger, as well as the fierce assaults of the besiegers, had made dire ravages in the place. The garrison's provisions of corn and cattle, their very horses, dogs, and donkeys had been eaten up – so that it might well be said by Wamba 'that famine, as well as slaughter, had *thinned* the garrison.' When the men of Chalus came on the walls to defend it against the scaling parties of King Richard – they were like so many skeletons in armour – they could hardly pull their bow-strings at last, or pitch down stones on the heads of His Majesty's party, so weak had their arms become. And the gigantic Count of Chalus, a warrior as redoubtable for his size and strength as Richard Plantagenet himself, was scarcely able to lift up his battleaxe upon the day of that last assault, when Sir Wilfrid of Ivanhoe ran him through the —. But we are advancing matters.

What should prevent me from describing the agonies of hunger which the count (a man of large appetite) suffered in company with his heroic sons and garrison? Nothing but that Dante has already done the business in the notorious history of Count Ugolino, so that my efforts might be considered as mere imitations. Why should I not, if I were minded to revel in horrifying details, show you how the famished garrison drew lots, and ate themselves during the siege; and how the unlucky lot falling upon the Countess of

35

Chalus, that heroic woman, taking an affectionate leave of her family, caused her large cauldron in the castle kitchen to be set a-boiling, had onions, carrots and herbs, pepper and salt made ready to make a savoury soup, as the French like it, and when all things were quite completed, kissed her children, jumped into the cauldron from off the kitchen stool and so was stewed down in her flannel bedgown? Dear friends, it is not from want of imagination, or from having no turn for the terrible or pathetic, that I spare you these details. I could give you some description that would spoil your dinner and night's rest, and make your hair stand on end. But why harrow your feelings? Fancy all the tortures and horrors that possibly can occur in a belea-guered and famished castle. Fancy the feelings of men who know that no more quarter will be given them than they would get if they were peaceful Hungarian citizens kidnapped and brought to trial by His Majesty the Emperor of Austria, and then let us rush on to the breach and prepare once more to meet the assault of dreadful King Richard and his men.

On the 29th of March in the year 1199, the good King, having copiously partaken of breakfast, caused his trumpets to blow and advanced with his host upon the breach of the castle of Chalus. Arthur de Pendennis bore his banner, Wilfrid of Ivanhoe fought on the King's right hand. Molyneux, Bishop of Bullocksmithy, doffed crosier and mitre for that day, and though fat and pursy, panted up the breach with the most resolute spirit, roaring out war cries and curses, and wielding a prodigious mace of iron, with which he did good execution. Hugo de Backbite was forced to come in attendance upon the Sovereign, but took care to keep in the rear of his august master, and to shelter behind his huge triangular shield as much as possible. Many lords of note followed the King and bore the ladders, and as they were placed against the wall, the air was perfectly dark with the showers of arrows which the French archers poured out at the besiegers, and the cataract of stones, kettles, bootjacks, chests of drawers, crockery, umbrellas, congreve-rockets, bombshells, bolts and arrows, and other missiles which the desperate garrison flung out on the storming party. The King received a copper coal-scuttle right over his eyes, and a mahogany wardrobe was discharged at his morion, which would have felled an ox, and would have done for the King had not Ivanhoe warded it off skilfully. Still they advanced, the warriors falling around them like grass beneath the scythe of the mower.

The ladders were placed in spite of the hail of death raining round: the King and Ivanhoe were, of course, the first to mount them. Chalus stood in the breach, borrowing strength from despair, and roaring out, 'Ha! Plantagenet, Saint Barbacue for Chalus!' He dealt the King a crack across the helmet with his battleaxe which shore off the gilt lion and crown that surmounted the steel cap. The King bent and reeled back; the besiegers were dismayed; the garrison and the Count of Chalus set up a shout of triumph: but it was premature.

As quick as thought Ivanhoe was into the count with a thrust in tierce, which took him just at the joint of the armour, and ran him through as clean as a spit does a partridge. Uttering a horrid shriek, he fell back writhing. The King, recovering, staggered up the parapet. The rush of knights followed, and the Union Jack was planted triumphantly on the walls, just as Ivanhoe... but we must leave him for a moment.

'Ha, St Richard! – ha, St George!' the tremendous voice of the Lion-king was heard over the loudest roar of the onset. At every sweep of his blade a severed head flew over the parapet, a spouting trunk tumbled, bleeding, on the flags of the bartizan. The world hath never seen a warrior equal to that lion-hearted Plantagenet as he raged over the keep, his eyes flashing fire through the bars of his morion, snorting and chafing with the hot lust of battle. One by one *les enfants de Chalus* had fallen: there was only one left at last of all the brave race that had fought round the gallant count – only one, and but a boy, a fair-headed boy, a blue-eyed boy! He had been gathering pansies in the fields but yesterday – it was but a few years, and he was a baby in his mother's arms! What could his puny sword do against the most redoubted blade in Christendom? – And yet Bohemond faced the great champion of England, and met him foot to foot! Turn away, turn away, my dear young friends and kind-hearted ladies! Do not look at that ill-fated poor boy! His blade is crushed into splinters under the axe of the conqueror, and the poor child is beaten to his knee!...

'Now, by St Barbacue of Limoges,' said Bertrand de Gourdon, 'the butcher will never strike down yonder lambling! Hold thy hand, Sir King, or, by St Barbacue –'

Swift as thought the veteran archer raised his arbalest to his shoulder – the whizzing bolt fled from the ringing string, and the next moment crushed quivering into the corslet of the Plantagenet.

It was a luckless shot, Bertrand de Gourdon! Maddened

by the pain of the wound, the brute nature of Richard was aroused: his fiendish appetite for blood rose to madness, and grinding his teeth, and with a curse too horrible to mention, the flashing axe of the royal butcher fell down on the blond ringlets of the child, and the children of Chalus were no more!...

I just throw this off by way of description, and to show what *might* be done if I chose to indulge in this style of composition, but as in the battles which are described by the kindly chronicler of one of whose works this present masterpiece is professedly a continuation everything passes off agreeably – the people are slain, but without any unpleasant sensation to the reader, nay, some of the most savage and blood-stained characters of history, such is the indomitable good humour of the great novelist, become amiable, jovial companions for whom one has a hearty sympathy – so, if you please, we will have this fighting business at Chalus, and the garrison and honest Bertrand of Gourdon disposed of, the former according to the usage of the good old times, having been hung up or murdered to a man, and the latter killed in the manner described by the late Dr Goldsmith in his History.

As for the Lion-hearted, we all very well know that the shaft of Bertrand de Gourdon put an end to the royal hero – and that from the 29th of March he never robbed or murdered any more. And we have legends in recondite books of the manner of the King's death.

'You must die, my son,' said the venerable Walter of Rouen, as Berengaria was carried shrieking from the King's tent.

'Repent, Sir King, and separate yourself from your children!'

'It is ill jesting with a dying man,' replied the King. 'Children have I none, my good lord bishop, to inherit after me.'

'Richard of England,' said the Archbishop, turning up his fine eyes, 'your vices are your children. Ambition is your eldest child, Cruelty is your second child, Luxury is your third child, and you have nourished them from your youth up. Separate yourself from these sinful ones, and prepare your soul, for the hour of departure draweth nigh.'

Violent, wicked, sinful as he might have been, Richard of England met his death like a Christian man. Peace be to the soul of the brave! When the news came to King Philip of France, he sternly forbade his courtiers to rejoice at the death of his enemy. 'It is no matter of joy but of dolour,' he said, 'that the bulwark of Christendom and the bravest king of Europe is no more.'

Meanwhile what had become of Sir Wilfrid of Ivanhoe, whom we left in the act of rescuing his Sovereign by running the Count of Chalus through the body?

As the good knight stooped down to pick his sword out of the corpse of his fallen foe, someone coming behind him suddenly thrust a dagger into his back at a place where his shirt of mail was open (for Sir Wilfrid had armed that morning in a hurry, and it was his breast, not his back, that he was accustomed ordinarily to protect); and when poor Wamba came up on the rampart, which he did when the fighting was over – being such a fool that he could not be got to thrust his head into danger for glory's sake – he found his dear knight with the dagger in his back lying without life upon the body of the Count de Chalus whom he had anon slain.

Ah! what a howl poor Wamba set up when he found his master killed! How he lamented over the corpse of that noble knight and friend! What mattered it to him that Richard the King was borne wounded to his tent, and that Bertrand de Gourdon was flayed alive? At another time the sight of this spectacle might have amused the simple knave; but now all his thoughts were of his lord, so good, so kind, so loyal, so frank with the great, so tender to the poor, so truthful of speech, so modest regarding his own merit, so true a gentlemen, in a word, that anybody might, with reason, deplore him.

As Wamba opened the dear knight's corslet, he found a locket round his neck, in which there was some hair, not flaxen like that of my Lady Rowena, who was almost as fair as an albino, but as black, Wamba thought, as the locks of the Jewish maiden whom the knight had rescued in the lists of Templestowe. A bit of Rowena's hair was in Sir Wilfrid's possession, too, but that was in his purse along with his seal of arms and a couple of groats; for the good knight never kept any money, so generous was he of his largesses when money came in.

Wamba took the purse, and seal, and groats, but he left the locket of hair round his master's neck, and when he returned to England never said a word about the circumstance. After all, how should he know whose hair it was? It might have been the knight's grandmother's hair for aught the fool knew, so he kept his counsel when he brought back the sad news and tokens to the disconsolate widow at Rotherwood.

The poor fellow would never have left the body at all, and indeed sat by it all night, and until the grey of the morning, when, seeing two suspicious-looking characters advancing towards him, he fled in dismay, supposing that they were marauders who were out searching for booty among the dead bodies; and having not the least courage, he fled from these, and tumbled down the breach, and never stopped running as fast as his legs would carry him until he reached the tents of his late beloved master.

The news of the knight's demise, it appeared, had been known at his quarters long before, for his servants were gone, and had ridden off on his horses. His chests were plundered, there was not so much as a shirt-collar left in his drawers, and the very bed and blankets had been carried away by these *faithful* attendants. Who had slain Ivanhoe? That remains a mystery to the present day; but Hugo de Backbite, whose nose he had pulled for defamation, and who was behind him in the assault of Chalus, was seen two years afterwards at the Court of King John in an embroidered velvet waistcoat which Rowena could have sworn she had worked for Ivanhoe, and about which the widow would have made some little noise but that – but that she was no longer a widow.

That she truly deplored the death of her lord cannot be questioned, for she ordered the deepest mourning which any milliner in York could supply, and erected a monument to his memory as big as a minster. But she was a lady of such fine principles that she did not allow her grief to overmaster her, and an opportunity speedily arising for uniting the two best Saxon families in England by an alliance between herself and the gentleman who offered himself to her, Rowena sacrificed her inclination to remain single to her sense of duty, and contracted a second matrimonial engagement.

That Athelstane was the man, I suppose no reader familiar with life and novels (which are a rescript of life, and are all strictly natural and edifying) can for a moment doubt. Cardinal Pandulfo tied the knot for them, and lest there should be any doubt about Ivanhoe's death (for his body was never sent home after all, nor seen after Wamba ran away from it), His Eminence procured a papal decree annulling the former marriage, so that Rowena became Mrs Athelstane with a clear conscience. And who shall be surprised if she was happier with the stupid and boozy thane than with the gentle and melancholy Wilfrid? Did women never have a predilection for fools, I should like to know, or fall in love with donkeys before the time of the amours of Bottom and Titania? 'Ah! Mary, had you not preferred an ass to a man, would you have married Jack Bray when a Michael Angelo offered? Ah! Fanny, were you not a woman, would you persist in adoring Tom Hiccups, who beats you and comes home tipsy from the club?' Yes, Rowena cared a hundred times more about tipsy Athelstane than ever she had done for gentle Ivanhoe, and so great was her infatuation about the latter that she would sit upon his knee in the presence of all her maidens, and let him smoke his cigar in the very drawing-room.

This is the epitaph she caused to be written by Father Drono (who piqued himself upon his Latinity) on the stone commemorating the death of her late lord:

Hic est Guilfridus, belli dum vixit avidus;
Cum gladio et lancea, Normannia et quoque Francia
Verbera dura dabat: per Turcos multum equitabat:
Guilbertum occidit: atque Hierosolyma vidit.
Heu! nunc sub fossa sunt tanti militis ossa,
Uxor Athelstani est conjux castissima Thani.

And this is the translation which the doggerel knave Wamba
made of the Latin lines:

Requiescat

Under the stone you behold,
Buried, and coffined, and cold,
Lieth Sir Wilfrid the Bold.

Always he marched in advance,
Warring in Flanders and France,
Doughty with sword and with lance.

Famous in Saracen fight,
Rode in his youth the good knight,
Scattering Paynims in flight.

Brian the Templar untrue,
Fairly in tourney he slew,
Saw Hierusalem too.

Now he is buried and gone,
Lying beneath the grey stone:
Where shall you find such a one?

Long time his widow deplored,
Weeping the fate of her lord.
Sadly cut off by the sword.

When she was eased of her pain,
Came the good Lord Athelstane,
When her ladyship married again.

Athelstane burst into a loud laugh when he heard it, at the last line, but Rowena would have had the fool whipped, had not the thane interceded – and to him, she said, she could refuse nothing.

CHAPTER IV

Ivanhoe redivivus

I trust nobody will suppose, from the events described in the last chapter, that our friend Ivanhoe is really dead. Because we have given him an epitaph or two and a monument, are these any reasons that he should be really gone out of the world? No: as in the pantomime, when we see Clown and Pantaloon lay out Harlequin and cry over him, we are always sure that Master Harlequin will be up at the next minute alert and shining in his glistening coat; and, after giving a box on the ears to the pair of them, will be taking a dance with Columbine, or leaping gaily through the clock-face, or into the three-pair-of-stairs window – so Sir Wilfrid, the Harlequin of our Christmas piece, may be run through a little, or may make believe to be dead, but will assuredly rise up again when he is wanted, and show himself at the right moment.

The suspicious-looking characters from whom Wamba ran away were no cutthroats and plunderers, as the poor knave imagined, but no other than Ivanhoe's friend, the hermit, and a revered brother of his, who visited the scene of the late battle in order to see if any Christians still survived there, whom they might shrive and get ready for heaven, or to whom they might possibly offer the benefit of their skill as leeches. Both were prodigiously learned in the healing art, and had about them those precious elixirs which so often occur in romances, and with which patients are so miraculously restored. Abruptly dropping his master's head from his lap as he fled, poor Wamba caused the knight's pate to fall with rather a heavy thump to the ground, and if the knave had but stayed a minute longer, he would have heard Sir Wilfrid utter a deep groan. But though the fool heard him not, the holy hermits did; and to recognise the gallant Wilfrid, to withdraw the enormous dagger still sticking out of his back, to wash the wound with a portion of the precious elixir, and to pour a little of it down his throat, was with the excellent hermits the work of an instant; which remedies being applied, one of the good men took the knight by the heels and the other by the head, and bore him daintily from the castle to their hermitage in a neighbouring rock. As for the Count of Chalus and the remainder of the slain, the hermits were too much occupied with Ivanhoe's case to mind them, and did not, it appears, give them any elixir, so that, if they are really dead, they must stay on the rampart stark and cold, or if otherwise, when the scene closes upon them as it does now, they may get up, shake themselves, go to the slips and drink a pot of porter, or change their stage-clothes and go home to supper. My dear readers, you may settle the matter among yourselves as you like. If you wish to kill the characters really off, let them be dead, and have done with them: but, *entre nous*, I don't believe they are any more dead than you or I are, and sometimes doubt whether there is a single syllable of truth in this whole story.

Well, Ivanhoe was taken to the hermits' cell, and there doctored by the holy fathers for his hurts, which were of such a severe and dangerous order that he was under medical treatment for a very considerable time. When he woke up from his delirium, and asked how long he had been ill, fancy his astonishment when he heard that he had been in the fever for six years! He thought the reverend fathers were joking at first, but their profession forbade them from that sort of levity; and besides, he could not possibly have got well any sooner, because the story would have been sadly put out had he appeared earlier. And it proves how good the fathers were to him, and how very nearly that scoundrel of a Hugh de Backbite's dagger had finished him, that he did not get well under this great length of time, during the whole of which the fathers tended him without ever thinking of a fee. I know of a kind physician in this town who does as much sometimes, but I won't do him the ill service of mentioning his name here.

Ivanhoe, being now quickly pronounced well, trimmed his beard, which by this time hung down considerably below his knees, and calling for his suit of chain armour, which before had fitted his elegant person as tight as wax, now put it on, and it bagged and hung so loosely about him that even the good friars laughed at his absurd appearance. It was impossible that he should go about the country in such a garb as that: the very boys would laugh at him. So the friars gave him one of their old gowns, in which he disguised himself; and, after taking an affectionate farewell of his friends, set forth on his return to his native country. As he went along, he learned that Richard was dead, that John reigned, that Prince Arthur had been poisoned, and was of course made acquainted with various other facts of public importance recorded in Pinnock's Catechism and the Historic Page.

But these subjects did not interest him near so much as his own private affairs, and I can fancy that his legs trembled under him, and his pilgrim's staff shook with emotion, as at length, after many perils, he came in sight of his paternal mansion of Rotherwood, and saw once more the chimneys smoking, the shadows of the oaks over the grass in the sunset, and the rooks winging over the trees. He heard the supper gong sounding: he knew his way to the door well enough. He entered the familiar hall with a benedicite, and without any more words took his place.

You might have thought for a moment that the grey friar trembled, and his shrunken cheek looked deadly pale, but he recovered himself presently, nor could you see his pallor for the cowl which covered his face.

A little boy was playing on Athelstane's knee. Rowena, smiling and patting the Saxon thane fondly on his broad bull-head, filled him a huge cup of spiced wine from a golden jug. He drained a quart of the liquor and, turning round, addressed the friar:

'And so, grey frere, thou sawest good King Richard fall at Chalus by the bolt of that felon bowman?'

'We did, an it please you. The brothers of our house attended the good King in his last months. In truth, he made a Christian ending!'

'And didst thou see the archer flayed alive? It must have been rare sport,' roared Athelstane, laughing hugely at the joke. 'How the fellow must have howled!'

'My love!' said Rowena, interposing tenderly, and putting a pretty white finger on his lip.

'I would have liked to see it too,' cried the boy.

'That's my own little Cedric, and so thou shalt. And, friar, didst see my poor kinsman Sir Wilfrid of Ivanhoe? They say he fought well at Chalus!'

'My sweet lord,' again interposed Rowena, 'mention him not.'

'Why? Because thou and he were so tender in days of yore – when you could not bear my plain face, being all in love with his pale one?'

'Those times are past now, dear Athelstane,' said his affectionate wife, looking up to the ceiling.

'Marry, thou never couldst forgive him the Jewess, Rowena.'

'The odious hussy! don't mention the name of the unbelieving creature,' exclaimed the lady.

'Well, well, poor Will was a good lad – a thought melancholy and milksop though. Why, a pint of sack fuddled his poor brains.'

'Sir Wilfrid of Ivanhoe was a good lance,' said the friar. 'I have heard there was none better in Christendom. He lay in our convent after his wounds, and it was there we tended him till he died. He was buried in our north cloister.'

'And there's an end of him,' said Athelstane. 'But come, this is dismal talk. Where's Wamba the jester? Let us have a song. Stir up, Wamba, and don't lie like a dog in the fire! Sing us a song, thou crack-brained jester, and leave off whimpering for bygones. Tush, man! There be many good fellows left in this world.'

'There be buzzards in eagles' nests,' Wamba said, who was lying stretched before the fire, sharing the hearth with the thane's dogs. 'There be dead men alive and live men dead. There be merry songs and dismal songs. Marry, and the merriest are the saddest sometimes. I will leave off motley and wear black, gossip Athelstane. I will turn howler at funerals, and then perhaps I shall be merry. Motley is fit for mutes, and black for fools. Give me some drink, gossip, for my voice is as cracked as my brain.'

'Drink and sing, thou beast, and cease prating,' the thane said.

And Wamba, touching his rebec wildly, sat up in the chimney-side and curled his lean shanks together and began:

Love at two score

Ho! pretty page with dimpled chin
That never has known the barber's shear,
All your aim is woman to win.
That is the way that boys begin.
Wait till you've come to forty year!

Curly gold locks cover foolish brains,
Billing and cooing is all your cheer,
Sighing and singing of midnight strains
Under Bonnybells' window-panes.
Wait till you've come to forty year!

Forty times over let Michaelmas pass,
Grizzling hair the brain doth clear;
Then you know a boy is an ass,
Then you know the worth of a lass,
Once you have come to forty year.

Pledge me round, I bid ye declare,
All good fellows whose beards are grey;
Did not the fairest of the fair

Common grow and wearisome, ere
Ever a month was past away?

The reddest lips that ever have kissed,
The brightest eyes that ever have shone,
May pray and whisper and we not list,
Or look away and never be missed,
Ere yet ever a month was gone.

Gillian's dead, Heaven rest her bier,
How I loved her twenty years syne!
Marian's married, but I sit here,
Alive and merry at forty year,
Dipping my nose in the Gascon wine.

'Who taught thee that merry lay, Wamba, thou son of Witless?' roared Athelstane, clattering his cup on the table and shouting the chorus.

'It was a good and holy hermit, sir, the pious clerk of Copmanhurst, that you wot of, who played many a prank with us in the days that we knew King Richard. Ah, noble sir, that was a jovial time and a good priest.'

'They say the holy priest is sure of the next bishopric, my love,' said Rowena. 'His Majesty hath taken him into much favour. My Lord of Huntingdon looked very well at the last ball, though I never could see any beauty in the countess – a freckled, blowzy thing, whom they used to call Maid Marian; though, for the matter of that, what between her flirtations with Major Littlejohn and Captain Scarlett, really –'

'Jealous again – haw! haw!' laughed Athelstane.

'I am above jealousy, and scorn it,' Rowena answered, drawing herself up very majestically.

'Well, well, Wamba's was a good song,' Athelstane said.

'Nay, a wicked song,' said Rowena, turning up her eyes as usual. 'What! rail at woman's love? Prefer a filthy wine cup to a true wife? Woman's love is eternal, my Athelstane. He who questions it would be a blasphemer were he not a fool. The well-born and well-nurtured gentlewoman loves once and once only.'

'I pray you, madam, pardon me, I – I am not well,' said the grey friar, rising abruptly from his settle, and tottering down the steps of the dais. Wamba sprung after him, his bells jingling as he rose, and casting his arms round the apparently fainting man he led him away into the court. 'There be dead men alive and live men dead,' whispered he. 'There be coffins to laugh at and marriages to cry over. Said I not sooth, holy friar?' And when they had got out into the solitary court, which was deserted by all the followers of the thane who were mingling in the drunken revelry in the hall, Wamba, seeing that none were by, knelt down, and kissing the friar's garment said, 'I knew thee, I knew thee, my lord and my liege!'

'Get up,' said Wilfrid of Ivanhoe, scarcely able to articulate. 'Only fools are faithful.'

And he passed on and into the little chapel where his father lay buried. All night long the friar spent there, and Wamba the Jester lay outside watching as mute as the saint over the porch.

When the morning came, Wamba was gone; and the knave being in the habit of wandering hither and thither as he chose, little notice was taken of his absence by a master and mistress who had not much sense of humour. As for Sir Wilfrid, a gentleman of his delicacy of feelings could not be expected to remain in a house where things so naturally disagreeable to him were occurring, and he quitted Rotherwood incontinently after paying a dutiful visit to the tomb where his old father, Cedric, was buried, and hastened on to York, at which city he made himself known to the family attorney, a most respectable man, in whose hands his ready money was deposited, and took up a sum sufficient to fit himself out with credit, and a handsome retinue, as became a knight of consideration. But he changed his name, wore a wig and spectacles, and disguised himself entirely, so that it was impossible his friends or the public should know him, and thus metamorphosed went about whithersoever his fancy led him. He was present at a public ball at York, which the Lord Mayor gave, where danced Sir Roger de Coverley in the very same set with Rowena – who was disgusted that Maid Marian took precedence of her – he saw little Athelstane overeat himself at the supper, and pledged his big father in a cup of sack; he met the Reverend Tuck at a missionary meeting, where he seconded a resolution proposed by that eminent divine. In fine, he saw a score of his old acquaintances, none of whom recognised in him the warrior of Palestine and Templestowe. Having a large fortune and nothing to do, he went about his country performing charities, slaying robbers, rescuing the distressed, and achieving noble feats of arms. Dragons and giants existed in his day no more, or be sure he would have had a fling at them: for the truth is, Sir Wilfrid of Ivanhoe was somewhat sick of the life which the hermits of Chalus had restored to him, and felt himself so friendless and solitary that he would not have been sorry to come to an end of it. Ah, my dear friends and intelligent British public, are there not others who are melancholy under a mask of gaiety, and who, in the midst of crowds, are lonely? Liston was a most melancholy man; Grimaldi had feelings; and there are others I wot of – but psha! – let us have the next chapter.

CHAPTER V

Ivanhoe to the rescue

The rascally manner in which the chicken-livered successor of Richard of the Lion-heart conducted himself to all parties – to his relatives, to his nobles, and his people – is a matter notorious, and set forth clearly in the Historic Page: hence, although nothing except perhaps success can, in my opinion, excuse disaffection to the Sovereign, or appearance in armed rebellion against him, the loyal reader will make allowance for two of the principal personages of the narrative, who will have to appear in the present chapter in the odious character of rebels to their lord and king. It must be remembered, in partial exculpation of the fault of Ivanhoe and Rowena (a fault for which they were bitterly punished, as you shall presently hear), that the monarch exasperated his subjects in a variety of ways – that before he murdered his royal nephew, Prince Arthur, there was a great question whether he was the rightful King of England at all – that his behaviour as an uncle and a family man was likely to wound the feelings of any lady and mother – finally, that there were palliations for the conduct of Rowena and Ivanhoe, which it now becomes our duty to relate.

When His Majesty destroyed Prince Arthur, the Lady Rowena, who was one of the ladies of honour to the Queen, gave up her place at Court at once, and retired to her castle of Rotherwood. Expressions made use of by her, and derogatory to the character of the Sovereign, were carried to the monarch's ears by some of those parasites, doubtless, by whom it is the curse of kings to be attended; and John swore, by St Peter's teeth, that he would be revenged upon the haughty Saxon lady – a kind of oath which, though he did not trouble himself about all other oaths, he was never known to break. It was not for some years after he had registered this vow that he was enabled to keep it.

Had Ivanhoe been present at Rouen when the King meditated his horrid designs against his nephew, there is little doubt that Sir Wilfrid would have prevented them, and rescued the boy. For Ivanhoe was, we need scarcely say, a hero of romance; and it is the custom and duty of all gentlemen of that profession to be present on all occasions of historic interest, to be engaged in all conspiracies, royal interviews, and remarkable occurrences – and hence Sir Wilfrid would certainly have rescued the young Prince, had he been anywhere in the neighbourhood of Rouen, where the foul tragedy occurred. But he was a couple of hundred leagues off, at Chalus, when the circumstance happened, tied down in his bed as crazy as a Bedlamite, and raving ceaselessly in the Hebrew tongue (which he had caught up during a previous illness in which he was tended by a maiden of that nation) about a certain Rebecca Ben Isaacs, of whom, being a married man, he would never have thought, had he been in his sound senses. During this delirium, what were politics to him, or he to politics? King John or King Arthur were entirely indifferent to a man who announced to his nurse-tenders, the good hermits of Chalus before mentioned, that he was the Marquis of Jericho, and about to marry Rebecca the Queen of Sheba. In a word, he only heard of what had occurred when he reached England, and his senses were restored to him. Whether was he happier, sound of brain and entirely miserable (as any man would be who found so admirable a wife as Rowena married again), or perfectly crazy, the husband of the beautiful Rebecca? I don't know which he liked best.

Howbeit the conduct of King John inspired Sir Wilfrid with so thorough a detestation of that Sovereign that he never could be brought to service under him, to get himself presented at St James's, or in any way to acknowledge, but by stern acquiescence, the authority of the sanguinary successor of his beloved King Richard. It was Sir Wilfrid of Ivanhoe, I need scarcely say, who got the barons of England to league together and extort from the King that famous instrument and palladium of our liberties at present in the British Museum, Great Russell Street, Bloomsbury – the Magna Carta. His name does not naturally appear in the list of barons, because he was only a knight, and a knight in disguise too: nor does Athelstane's signature figure on that document. Athelstane, in the first place, could not write; nor did he care a pennypiece about politics, so long as he could drink his wine at home undisturbed and have his hunting and shooting in quiet.

It was not until the King wanted to interfere with the sport of every gentleman in England (as we know by reference to the Historic Page that this odious monarch did), that Athelstane broke out into open rebellion, along with several Yorkshire squires and noblemen. It is recorded of the King that he forbade every man to hunt his own deer; and, in order to secure an obedience to his orders, this Herod of a monarch wanted to secure the eldest sons of all the nobility and gentry as hostages for the good behaviour of their parents.

Athelstane was anxious about his game; Rowena was anxious about her son. The former swore that he would hunt his deer in spite of all Norman tyrants; the latter asked, should she give up her boy to the ruffian who had murdered his own nephew?[1] The speeches of both were brought to the King at York; and, furious, he ordered an instant attack upon Rotherwood, and that the lord and lady of that castle should be brought before him dead or alive.

Ah, where was Wilfrid of Ivanhoe, the unconquerable champion, to defend the castle against the royal party? A few thrusts from his lance would have spitted the leading warriors of the King's host, a few cuts from his sword would have put John's forces to rout. But the lance and sword of Ivanhoe were idle on this occasion. 'No, be hanged to me!' said the knight bitterly, '*this* is a quarrel in which I can't interfere. Common politeness forbids. Let yonder ale-swilling Athelstane defend his – ha, ha – *wife*; and my Lady Rowena guard her – ha, ha – *son*.' And he laughed wildly and madly, and the sarcastic way in which he choked and gurgled out the words 'wife' and 'son' would have made you shudder to hear.

When he heard, however, that on the fourth day of the siege Athelstane had been slain by a cannon-ball (and this time for good, and not to come to life again as he had done before), and that the widow (if so the innocent bigamist may be called) was conducting the defence of Rotherwood herself with the greatest intrepidity, showing herself upon the walls with her little son (who bellowed like a bull, and did not like the fighting at all), pointing the guns and

1. See Hume, Giraldus Cambrensis, The Monk of Croyland, and Pinnock's Catechism.

encouraging the garrison in every way – better feelings returned to the bosom of the Knight of Ivanhoe, and summoning his men, he armed himself quickly, and determined to go forth to the rescue.

He rode without stopping for two days and two nights in the direction of Rotherwood, with such swiftness and disregard for refreshment, indeed, that his men dropped one by one upon the road, and he arrived alone at the lodge-gate of the park. The windows were smashed, the door stove in; the lodge, a neat little Swiss cottage with a garden where the pinafores of Mrs Gurth's children might have been seen hanging on the gooseberry bushes in more peaceful times, was now a ghastly heap of smoking ruins – cottage, bushes, pinafores, children lay mangled together, destroyed by the licentious soldiery of an infuriate monarch! Far be it from me to excuse the disobedience of Athelstane and Rowena to their Sovereign, but surely – surely this cruelty might have been spared.

Gurth, who was lodge-keeper, was lying dreadfully wounded and expiring at the flaming and violated threshold of his lately picturesque home. A catapult and a couple of mangonels had done his business. The faithful fellow, recognising his master, who had put up his visor and forgotten his wig and spectacles in the agitation of the moment, exclaimed, 'Sir Wilfrid! My dear master – praised be St Waltheof – there may be yet time – my beloved mistr... master Athelst...' He sank back, and never spoke again.

Ivanhoe spurred on his horse Bavieca madly up the chestnut avenue. The castle was before him, the western tower was in flames, the besiegers were pressing at the southern gate. Athelstane's banner, the bull rampant, was still on the northern bartizan. 'An Ivanhoe, an Ivanhoe!' he bellowed out, with a shout that overcame all the din of battle – *Nostre Dame a la rescousse* – and to hurl his lance through the midriff of Reginald de Bracy, who was commanding the assault, who fell howling with anguish, to wave his battleaxe over his own head, and cut off those of thirteen men-at-arms, was the work of an instant. 'An Ivanhoe, an Ivanhoe!' he still shouted, and down went a man as sure as he said 'Hoe!'

'Ivanhoe! Ivanhoe!' a shrill voice cried from the top of the northern bartizan. Ivanhoe knew it.

'Rowena! my love! I come!' he roared on his part. 'Villains! Touch but a hair of her head, and I...'

Here, with a sudden plunge and a squeal of agony, Bavieca sprang forward wildly, and fell as wildly on her back, rolling over and over upon the knight. All was dark before him – his brain reeled – it whizzed – something came crashing down on his forehead. St Waltheof and all the saints of the Saxon calendar, protect the knight!...

When he came to himself, Wamba and the lieutenant of his lances were leaning over him with a bottle of the hermit's elixir. 'We arrived here the day after the battle,' said the fool. 'Marry, I have a knack of that.'

'Your worship rode so deucedly quick, there was no keeping up with your worship,' said the lieutenant.

'The day... after... the bat...' groaned Ivanhoe. 'Where is the Lady Rowena?'

'The castle has been taken and sacked,' the lieutenant said – and pointed to what once *was* Rotherwood, but was now only a heap of smoking ruins. Not a tower was left, not a roof, not a floor, not a single human being! Everything was flame and ruin, smash and murder!

Of course Ivanhoe fell back fainting again among the ninety-seven men-at-arms whom he had slain, and it was not until Wamba had applied a second, and uncommonly strong, dose of the elixir that he came to life again. The good knight was, however, from long practice so accustomed to the severest wounds that he bore them far more easily than common folk, and thus was enabled to reach York upon a litter – which his men constructed for him – with tolerable ease.

Rumour had as usual advanced him, and he heard at the hotel where he stopped what had been the issue of the affair at Rotherwood. A minute or two after his horse was stabbed, and Ivanhoe knocked down, the western bartizan was taken by the storming party which invested it, and every soul slain, except Rowena and her boy, who were tied upon horses and carried away under a secure guard to one of the King's castles – nobody knew whither – and Ivanhoe was recommended by the hotel-keeper (whose house he had used in former times) to reassume his wig and spectacles, and not call himself by his own name any more, lest some of the King's people should lay hands on him. However, as he had killed everybody round about him, there was but little danger of his discovery, and the Knight of the Spectacles, as he was called, went about York quite unmolested, and at liberty to attend to his own affairs.

We wish to be brief in narrating this part of the gallant hero's existence, for his life was one of feeling rather than affection, and the description of mere sentiment is considered by many well-informed persons to be tedious. What *were* his sentiments, now it may be asked, under the peculiar position in which he found himself? He had done his duty by Rowena, certainly: no man could say otherwise. But as for being in love with her any more, after what had occurred, that was a different question. Well, come what would, he was determined still to continue doing his duty by her; but as she was whisked away, the deuce knew whither, how could he do anything? So he resigned himself to the fact that she was thus whisked away.

He, of course, sent emissaries about the country to endeavour to find out where Rowena was, but these came back without any sort of intelligence, and it was remarked that he still remained in a perfect state of resignation. He remained in this condition for a year or more, and it was said that he was becoming more cheerful, and he certainly was growing rather fat. The Knight of the Spectacles was voted an agreeable man in a grave way, and gave some very elegant, though quiet parties, and was received in the best society of York.

It was just at assize time, the lawyers and barristers had arrived, and the town was unusually gay, when one morning the attorney, whom we have mentioned as Sir Wilfrid's man of business, and a most respectable man, called upon his gallant client at his lodgings, and said he had a communication of importance to make. Having to communicate with a client of rank, who was condemned to be hanged for forgery, Sir Hugo de Backbite, the attorney said he had been to visit that party in the condemned cell, and on the way through the yard, and through the bars of another cell, had seen and recognised an old acquaintance of Sir Wilfrid of Ivanhoe – and the lawyer held him out, with a particular look, a note written on a piece of whity-brown paper.

What were Ivanhoe's sensations when he recognised the handwriting of Rowena! – He tremblingly dashed open the billet, and read as follows:

'My dearest Ivanhoe – for I am thine now as erst, and my first love for ever – ever dear to me. Have I been near thee dying for a whole year, and didst thou make no effort to rescue thy Rowena? Have ye given to others – I mention not their name nor their odious creed – the heart that ought to be mine? I send thee my forgiveness from my dying pallet of straw. I forgive thee the insults I have received, the cold and hunger I have endured, the failing health of my boy, the bitterness of my prison, thy infatuation about that Jewess, which made our married life miserable, and which caused thee, I am sure, to go abroad to look after her. I forgive thee all my wrongs, and fain would bid thee farewell. Mr Smith hath gained over my gaoler – he will tell thee how I may see thee. Come and console my last hour by promising that thou wilt care for my boy – his boy who fell like a hero (when thou wert absent) combating by the side of

– Rowena

The reader may consult his own feelings and say whether Ivanhoe was likely to be pleased or not by this letter. However, he enquired of Mr Smith the solicitor what was the plan which that gentleman had devised for the introduction to Lady Rowena, and was informed that he was to get a barrister's gown and wig, when the gaoler would introduce him into the interior of the prison. These decorations, knowing several gentlemen of the Northern Circuit, Sir Wilfrid of Ivanhoe easily procured, and, with feelings of no small trepidation, reached the cell where, for the space of a year, poor Rowena had been immured.

If any person have a doubt of the correctness, of the historical exactness, of this narrative, I refer him to the *Biographie Universelle* (article 'Jean sans Terre'), which says, '*La femme d'un baron auquel on vint demander son fils, répondit, "Le roi pense-t-il que je confierai mon fils à un homme qui a égorgé son neveu de sa propre main?" Jean fit enlever la mère et l'enfant, et la laissa mourir de faim dans les cachots.*'

I picture to myself, with a painful sympathy, Rowena undergoing this disagreeable sentence. All her virtues, her resolution, her chaste energy and perseverance, shine with redoubled lustre, and, for the first time since the commencement of the history, I feel that I am partially reconciled to her. The weary year passes – she grows weaker and more languid, thinner and thinner! At length Ivanhoe, in the disguise of a barrister of the Northern Circuit, is introduced into her cell, and finds his lady in the last stages of exhaustion, on the straw of her dungeon, with her little boy in her arms. She has preserved his life at the expense of her own, giving him the whole of the pittance which her gaolers allowed her, and perishing herself of inanition.

There is a scene! I feel as if I had made it up, as it were, with this lady, and that we part in peace, in consequence of my providing her with so sublime a deathbed. Fancy Ivanhoe's entrance – their recognition – the faint blush upon her worn features – the pathetic way in which she gives little Cedric in charge to him, and his promises of protection.

'Wilfrid, my early loved,' slowly gasped she, removing her grey hair from her furrowed temples, and gazing on her boy fondly, as he nestled on Ivanhoe's knee, 'promise me, by St Waltheof of Templestowe – promise me one boon!'

'I do,' said Ivanhoe, clasping the boy, and thinking it was to that little innocent the promise was intended to apply.

'By St Waltheof?'

'By St Waltheof!'

'Promise me, then,' gasped Rowena, staring wildly at him, 'that you never will marry a Jewess.'

'By St Waltheof,' cried Ivanhoe, 'this is too much! Rowena!' But he felt his hand grasped for a moment, the nerves then relaxed, the pale lip ceased to quiver – she was no more!

CHAPTER VI

Ivanhoe the widower

Having placed young Cedric at school at the Hall of Dotheboyes in Yorkshire, and arranged his family affairs, Sir Wilfrid of Ivanhoe quitted a country which had no longer any charms for him, and in which his stay was rendered the less agreeable by the notion that King John would hang him if ever he could lay hands on the faithful follower of King Richard and Prince Arthur.

But there was always in those days a home and occupation for a brave and pious knight. A saddle on a gallant warhorse, a pitched field against the Moors, a lance wherewith to spit a turbaned infidel, or a road to Paradise carved out by his scimitar – these were the height of the ambition of good and religious warriors; and so renowned a champion as Sir Wilfrid of Ivanhoe was sure to be well received wherever blows were stricken for the cause of Christendom. Even among the dark Templars, he who had twice overcome the most famous lance of their Order was a respected though not a welcome guest. But, among the opposition company of the Knights of St John, he was admired and courted beyond measure; and always affectioning that Order, which offered him, indeed, its first rank and commanderies, he did much good service, fighting in their ranks for the glory of heaven and St Waltheof, and slaying many thousands of the heathen in Prussia, Poland, and those savage northern countries. The only fault that the great and gallant, though severe and ascetic Folko of Heydenbraten, the chief of the Order of

St John, found with the melancholy warrior, whose lance did such good service to the cause, was that he did not persecute the Jews as so religious a knight should. He let off sundry captives of that persuasion whom he had taken with his sword and his spear, saved others from torture, and actually ransomed the two last grinders of a venerable rabbi (that Roger de Cartright, an English Knight of the Order, was about to extort from the elderly Israelite) with a hundred crowns and a gimmal ring, which were all the property he possessed. Whenever he so ransomed or benefited one of this religion, he would moreover give them a little token or a message (were the good knight out of money), saying, 'Take this token, and remember this deed was done by Wilfrid the Disinherited, for the services whilome rendered to him by Rebecca, the daughter of Isaac of York.' So among themselves, and in their meetings and synagogues, and in their restless travels from land to land, when they of Jewry cursed and reviled all Christians, as such abominable heathens will, they nevertheless excepted the name of the Desdichado, or the doubly-disinherited as he now was, the Desdichado-Doblado.

The account of all the battles, storms, and escalades in which Sir Wilfrid took part would only weary the reader, for the chopping off one heathen's head with an axe must be very like the decapitation of any other unbeliever. Suffice it to say, that wherever this kind of work was to be done, and Sir Wilfrid was in the way, he was the man to perform it. It would astonish you were you to see the account that Wamba kept of his master's achievements, and of Bulgarians, Bohemians, Croatians slain or maimed by his hand. And as, in those days, a reputation for valour had an immense effect upon the soft hearts of women, and even the ugliest man, were he a stout warrior, was looked upon with favour by Beauty, so Ivanhoe, who was by no means ill-favoured, though now becoming rather elderly, made conquests over female breasts as well as over Saracens, and had more than one direct offer of marriage made to him by princesses, countesses, and noble ladies possessing both charms and money, which they were anxious to place at the disposal of a champion so renowned. It is related that the Duchess Regent of Kartoffelberg offered him her hand and the Ducal Crown of Kartoffelberg, which he had rescued from the unbelieving Prussians, but Ivanhoe evaded the Duchess' offer by riding away from her capital secretly at midnight, and hiding himself in a convent of Knights Hospitallers, on the borders of Poland. And it is a fact that the Princess Rosalia Seraphina of Pumpernickel, the most lovely woman of her time, became so frantically attached to him that she followed him on a campaign, and was discovered with his baggage disguised as a horse-boy. But no princess, no beauty, no female blandishments had any charms for Ivanhoe: no hermit practised a more austere celibacy. The severity of his morals contrasted so remark-ably with the lax and dissolute manner of the young lords and nobles in the courts which he frequented that these young springalds would sometimes sneer and call him 'Monk' and 'Milksop'. But his courage in the day of battle was so terrible and admirable that I promise you the youthful libertines did not sneer *then*, and the most reckless of them often turned pale when they couched their lances to follow Ivanhoe. Holy Waltheof! It was an awful sight to see him with his pale, calm face, his shield upon his breast, his heavy lance before him, charging a squadron of heathen Bohemians or a regiment of Cossacks! Wherever he saw the enemy, Ivanhoe assaulted him, and when people remonstrated with him, and said if he attacked such and such a post, breach, castle or army he would be slain, 'And suppose I be?' he answered, giving them to understand that he would as lief the battle of life were over altogether.

While he was thus making war against the northern infidels, news was carried all over Christendom of a catastrophe which had befallen the good cause in the south of Europe, where the Spanish Christians had met with such a defeat and massacre at the hands of the Moors as had never been known in the proudest days of Saladin.

Thursday the 9th of Shaban, in the 605th year of the Hegira, is known all over the west as the *amun-al-ark*, the year of the battle of Alarcos, gained over the Christians by the Muslims of Andalus, on which fatal day Christendom suffered a defeat so signal that it was feared the Spanish peninsula would be entirely wrested away from the dominion of the Cross. On that day the Franks lost 150,000 men and 30,000 prisoners. A man slave sold among the unbelievers for a dirham; a donkey, for the same; a sword, half a dirham; a horse, five dirhams. Hundreds of thousand of these various sorts of booty were in the possession of the triumphant followers of Yakoob al Mansoor. Curses on his head! But he was a brave warrior, and the Christians before him seemed to forget that they were the descendants of the brave Cid, the *Kanbitoor*, as the Moorish hounds (in their jargon) denominated the famous Campeador.

A general move for the rescue of the faithful in Spain – a

crusade against the infidels triumphing there, was preached throughout all Europe by all the most eloquent clergy: and thousands and thousands of valorous knights and nobles, accompanied by well-meaning varlets and vassals of the lower sort, trooped from all sides to the rescue. The straits of Gibel-al-Tariff, at which spot the Moor, passing from Barbary, first planted his accursed foot on the Christian soil, were crowded with the galleys of the Templars and the Knights of St John, who flung succours into the menaced kingdoms of the peninsula; the inland sea swarmed with their ships hasting from their forts and islands, from Rhodes and Byzantium, from Jaffa and Askalon. The Pyrenean peaks beheld the pennons and glittered with the armour of the knights marching out of France into Spain; and, finally, in a ship that set sail at the time when the news of the defeat of Alarcos came and alarmed all good Christians, Ivanhoe landed at Barcelona, and proceeded to slaughter the Moors forthwith.

He brought letters of introduction from his friend Folko of Heydenbraten, the Grand Master of the Knights of St John, to the venerable Baldomero de Garbanzos, Grand Master of the renowned order of Saint Jago. The chief of Saint Jago's knights paid the greatest respect to a warrior whose fame was already so widely known in Christendom, and Ivanhoe had the pleasure of being appointed to all the posts of danger and forlorn hopes that could be devised in his honour. He would be called up twice or thrice in a night to fight the Moors. He led ambushes, scaled breaches, was blown up by mines, was wounded many hundred times (recovering thanks to the elixir, of which Wamba always carried a supply). He was the terror of the Saracens, and the admiration and wonder of the Christians.

To describe his deeds would, I say, be tedious: one day's battle was like that of another. I am not writing in ten volumes like Monsieur Alexandre Dumas, or even in three like other great authors. We have no room for recounting of Sir Wilfrid's deeds of valour. Whenever he took a Moorish town, it was remarked that he went anxiously into the Jewish quarter, and enquired amongst the Hebrews – who were great in numbers in Spain – for Rebecca, the daughter of Isaac. Many Jews, according to his wont, he ransomed, and created so much scandal by this proceeding, and by the manifest favour which he showed to the people of the nation, that the Master of Saint Jago remonstrated with him, and it is probable he would have been cast into the Inquisition and roasted, but that his prodigious valour and success against the Moors counterbalanced his heretical partiality for the children of Jacob.

It chanced that the good knight was present at the siege of Xixona in Andalusia, entering the breach the first, according to his wont, and slaying, with his own hand, the Moorish lieutenant of the town and several hundred more of its unbelieving defenders. He had very nearly done for the Alfaqui, or governor, a veteran warrior with a crooked scimitar and a beard as white as snow, but a couple of hundred of the Alfaqui's bodyguard flung themselves between Ivanhoe and their chief, and the old fellow escaped with his life, leaving a handful of his beard in the grasp of the English knight. The strictly military business being done, and such of the garrison as did not escape put, as by right, to the sword, the good knight, Sir Wilfrid of Ivanhoe, took no further part in the proceedings of the conquerors of that ill-fated place. A scene of horrible massacre and frightful reprisals ensued, and the Christian warriors, hot with victory and flushed with slaughter, were, it is to be feared, as savage in their hour of triumph as ever their heathen enemies had been.

Amongst the most violent and least scrupulous was the ferocious knight of Saint Jago, Don Beltran de Cuchilla y Trabuco y Espada y Espelon. Raging through the vanquished city like a demon, he slaughtered indiscriminately all those infidels of both sexes whose wealth did not tempt him to a ransom, or whose beauty did not reserve them for more frightful calamities than death. The slaughter over, Don Beltran took up his quarters in the Albaycen, where the Alfaqui had lived who had so narrowly escaped the sword of Ivanhoe; but the wealth, the treasure, the slaves, and the family of the fugitive chieftain were left in possession of the conqueror of Xixona. Among the treasures, Don Beltran recognised with a savage joy the coat-armours and ornaments of many brave and unfortunate companions-in-arms who had fallen in the fatal battle of Alarcos. The sight of those bloody relics added fury to his cruel disposition, and served to steel a heart already but little disposed to sentiments of mercy.

Three days after the sack and plunder of the place, Don Beltran was seated in the hall-court lately occupied by the proud Alfaqui, lying in his divan, dressed in his rich robes, the fountains playing in the centre, the slaves of the Moor ministering to his scarred and rugged Christian conqueror. Some fanned him with peacocks' pinions, some danced before him, some sang Moors' melodies to the plaintive notes of a *guzla*, one – it was the only daughter of the

Moor's old age, the young Zutulbe, a rosebud of beauty – sat weeping in a corner of the gilded hall, weeping for her slain brethren, the pride of Muslim chivalry, whose heads were blackening in the blazing sunshine on the portals without, and for her father, whose home had been thus made desolate.

He and his guest, the English knight Sir Wilfrid, were playing at chess, a favourite amusement with the chivalry of the period, when a messenger was announced from Valencia, to treat, if possible, for the ransom of the remaining part of the Alfaqui's family. A grim smile lit up Don Beltran's features as he bade the black slave admit the messenger. He entered. By his costume it was at once seen that the bearer of the flag of truce was a Jew – the people were employed continually then as ambassadors between the two races at war in Spain.

'I come,' said the old Jew (in a voice which made Sir Wilfrid start), 'from my lord the Alfaqui to my noble señor, the invincible Don Beltran de Cuchilla, to treat for the ransom of the Moor's only daughter, the child of his old age and the pearl of his affection.'

'A pearl is a valuable jewel, Hebrew. What does the Moorish dog bid for her?' asked Don Beltran, still smiling grimly.

'The Alfaqui offers a hundred thousand dinars, twenty-four horses with their caparisons, twenty-four suits of plate-armour, and diamonds and rubies to the amount of a million dinars.'

'Ho, slaves!' roared Don Beltran, 'show the Jew my treasure of gold. How many hundred thousand pieces are there?' And ten enormous chests were produced in which the accountant counted a thousand bags of a thousand dirhams each, and displayed several caskets of jewels containing such a treasure of rubies, smaragds, diamonds, and jacinths as made the eyes of the aged ambassador twinkle with avarice.

'How many horses are there in my stable?' continued Don Beltran, and Muley, the master of the horse, numbered three hundred fully caparisoned; and there was, likewise, armour of the richest sort for as many cavaliers, who followed the banner of this doughty captain.

'I want neither money nor armour,' said the ferocious knight. 'Tell this to the Alfaqui, Jew. And I will keep the child, his daughter, to serve the messes for my dogs, and clean the platters for my scullions.'

'Deprive not the old man of his child,' here interposed the Knight of Ivanhoe. 'Bethink thee, brave Don Beltran, she is but an infant in years.'

'She is my captive, Sir Knight,' replied the surly Don Beltran. 'I will do with my own as becomes me.'

'Take two hundred thousand dirhams!' cried the Jew. 'More! anything! The Alfaqui will give his life for his child!'

'Come hither, Zutulbe! – Come hither, thou Moorish pearl!' yelled the ferocious warrior. 'Come closer, my pretty black-eyed houri of heathenesse! Hast heard the name of Beltran de Espada y Trabuco?'

'There were three brothers of that name at Alarcos, and my brothers slew the Christian dogs!' said the proud young girl, looking boldly at Don Beltran, who foamed with rage.

'The Moors butchered my mother and her little ones at midnight in our castle of Murcia,' Beltran said.

'Thy father fled like a craven, as thou didst, Don Beltran!'

cried the high-spirited girl.

'By Saint Jago, this is too much!' screamed the infuriated nobleman, and the next moment there was a shriek, and the maiden fell to the ground with Don Beltran's dagger in her side.

'Death is better than dishonour!' cried the child, rolling on the blood-stained marble pavement. 'I… I spit upon thee, dog of a Christian!' and with this, and with a savage laugh, she fell back and died.

'Bear back this news, Jew, to the Alfaqui,' howled the Don, spurning the beauteous corpse with his foot. 'I would not have ransomed her for all the gold in Barbary!' And shuddering, the old Jew left the apartment, which Ivanhoe quitted likewise.

When they were in the outer court, the knight said to the Jew, 'Isaac of York, dost thou not know me?' and threw back his hood, and looked at the old man.

The old Jew stared wildly, rushed forward, as if to seize his hand, then started back, trembling convulsively, and, clutching his withered hands over his face, said with a burst of grief, 'Sir Wilfrid of Ivanhoe! – No, no! – I do not know thee!'

'Holy mother! What has chanced?' said Ivanhoe, in his turn becoming ghastly pale. 'Where is thy daughter? – Where is Rebecca?'

'Away from me!' said the old Jew, tottering. 'Away! Rebecca is… dead!'

When the disinherited knight heard that fatal announcement, he fell to the ground senseless, and was for some days as one perfectly distraught with grief. He took no nourishment and uttered no word. For weeks he did not relapse out of his moody silence, and when he came partially to himself again, it was to bid his people to horse, in a hollow voice, and to make a foray against the Moors. Day after day he issued out against the infidels, and did nought but slay and slay. He took no plunder as other knights did, but left that to his followers. He uttered no war cry, as was the manner of chivalry, and he gave no quarter, insomuch that the 'silent knight' became the dread of all the Paynims of Granada and Andalusia, and more fell by his lance than by that of any of the most clamorous captain of the troops in arms against them. Thus the tide of battle turned, and the Arab historian El Makary recounts how, at the great battle of Al Akab, called by the Spaniards Las Navas, the Christians retrieved their defeat at Alarcos, and absolutely killed half a million of Mahometans. Fifty thousand of these, of course, Don Wilfrid took to his own lance, and it was remarked that the melancholy warrior seemed somewhat more easy in spirits after that famous feat of arms.

CHAPTER VII

The end of the performance

In a short time the redoubtable knight, Wilfrid of Ivanhoe, had killed off so many of the Moors that though those unbelieving miscreants poured continual reinforcements into Spain from Barbary, they could make no head against the Christian forces, and in fact came into battle quite discouraged at the notion of meeting the dreadful silent knight. It was commonly believed amongst them that the famous Malek Ric Richard of England, the conqueror of Saladin, had come to life again, and was battling in the Spanish hosts – that this, his second life, was a charmed one, and his body inaccessible to blow of scimitar or thrust of spear – that after battle he ate the hearts and drank the blood of many young Moors for his supper. A thousand wild legends were told of Ivanhoe, indeed, so that the Morisco warriors came half-vanquished into the field, and fell an easy prey to the Spaniards, who cut away among them without mercy. And although none of the Spanish historians whom I have consulted make mention of Sir Wilfrid as the real author of the numerous triumphs which now graced the arms of the good cause, this is not in the least to be wondered at in a nation that has always been notorious for bragging and for the non-payment of their debts of gratitude as of their other obligations, and that writes histories of the Peninsular war with the Emperor Napoleon without making the slightest mention of his Grace the Duke of Wellington, or of the part taken by British valour in that transaction. Well, it must be confessed on the other hand that we brag enough of our fathers' feats in those campaigns, but this is not the subject at present under consideration.

To be brief, Ivanhoe made such short work with the unbelievers that the monarch of Aragon, King Don Jayme, saw himself speedily enabled to besiege the city of Valencia, the last stronghold which the Moors had in his dominions, and garrisoned by many thousands of those infidels under the command of their King Aboo Abdallah Mahommed, son of Yakoob al Mansoor. The Arabian historian El Makary gives a full account of the military precautions taken by Aboo Abdallah to defend his city, but as I do not wish to make a parade of my learning, or to write a costume novel, I shall pretermit any description of the city under its Moorish governors.

Besides the Turks who inhabited it, there dwelt within its walls great store of those of the Hebrew nation, who were always protected by the Moors during their unbelieving reign in Spain, and who were, as we very well know, the chief physicians, the chief bankers, the chief statesmen, the chief artists and musicians, the chief everything, under the Moorish kings. Thus it is not surprising that the Hebrews, having their money, their liberty, their teeth, their lives secure under the Mahometan domination, should infinitely prefer it to the Christian sway, beneath which they were liable to be deprived of every one of these benefits.

Among these Hebrews of Valencia, lived a very ancient Israelite – no other than Isaac of York, before mentioned – who came into Spain with his daughter soon after Ivanhoe's marriage, in the third volume of the first part of this history. Isaac was respected by his people for the money which he possessed, and his daughter for her admirable good qualities, her beauty, her charities, and her remarkable medical skill.

The young Emir Aboo Abdallah was so struck by her charms that though she was considerably older than His Highness, he offered to marry her, and install her as number one of his wives – and Isaac of York would not have objected to the union (for such mixed marriages were not uncommon between the Hebrews and Moors those days) – but Rebecca firmly, but respectfully, declined the proposals of the Prince, saying it was impossible she should unite herself with a man of a creed different to her own.

Although Isaac was, probably, not overwell pleased at losing this chance of being father-in-law to a Royal Highness, yet as he passed among his people for a very strict character, and there were in his family several rabbis of great reputation and severity of conduct, the old gentleman was silenced by this opposition of Rebecca's, and the young lady herself applauded by her relatives for her resolute behaviour. She took their congratulations in a very frigid manner, and said that it was her wish not to marry at all, but to devote herself to the practice of medicine altogether, and to helping the sick and needy of her people. Indeed, although she did not go to any public meetings, she was as benevolent a creature as the world ever saw: the poor blessed her wherever they knew her, and many benefited by her who guessed not whence her gentle bounty came.[2]

But there are men in Jewry who admire beauty, and, as I

2. Though I am writing but a Christmas farce, I hope the kind-hearted reader will excuse me for saying that I am thinking of the beautiful life and death of Adelaide the Queen.

have even heard, appreciate money too, and Rebecca had such a quantity of both that all the most desirable bachelors of the people were ready to bid for her. Ambassadors came from all quarters to propose for her. Her own uncle, the venerable Ben Solomons, with a beard as long as a Kashmir goat, and a reputation for learning and piety which still lives in his nation, quarrelled with his son Moses, the red-haired diamond merchant of Trebizond, and his son Simeon, the bald bill-broker of Baghdad, each putting in a claim for their cousin. Ben Minories came from London, and knelt at her feet; Ben Jochanan arrived from Paris, and thought to dazzle her with the latest waistcoats from the Palais Royal; and Ben Jonah brought her a present of Dutch herrings, and besought her to come back and be Mrs Ben Jonah at the Hague.

Rebecca temporised as best she might. She thought her uncle was too old. She besought dear Moses and dear Simeon not to quarrel with each other, and offend their father by pressing their suit. Ben Minories from London, she said, was too young, and Jochanan from Paris, she pointed out to Isaac of York, must be a spendthrift, or he would not wear those absurd waistcoats. As for Ben Jonah, she said she could not bear the notion of tobacco and Dutch herrings – she wished to stay with her papa, her dear papa. In fine, she invented a thousand excuses for her delay, and it was plain that marriage was odious to her. The only man whom she received with anything like favour, was young Bevis Marks of London, with whom she was very familiar. But Bevis had come to her with a certain token that had been given to him by an English knight, who saved him from a faggot to which the ferocious Hospitaller Folko of

Heydenbraten was about to condemn him. It was but a ring, with an emerald in it that Bevis knew to be sham, and not worth a groat. Rebecca knew about the value of jewels too, but ah! she valued this one more than all the diamonds in Prester John's turban. She kissed it, she cried over it, she wore it in her bosom always; and when she knelt down at night and morning, she held it between her folded hands on her neck... Young Bevis Marks went away finally no better off than the others; the rascal sold to the King of France a handsome ruby, the very size of the bit of glass in Rebecca's ring, but he always said he would rather have had her than ten thousand pounds, and very likely he would, for it was known she would at once have a plumb to her fortune.

These delays, however, could not continue for ever, and at a great family meeting held at Passover time, Rebecca was solemnly ordered to choose a husband out of the gentlemen there present, her aunts pointing out the great kindness which had been shown to her by her father in permitting her to choose for herself. One aunt was of the Solomon faction, another aunt took Simeon's side, a third most venerable old lady – the head of the family, and a hundred and forty-four years of age – was ready to pronounce a curse upon her, and cast her out, unless she married before the month was over. All the jewelled heads of the old ladies in council, all the beards of all the family wagged against her – it must have been an awful sight to witness.

At last, then, Rebecca was forced to speak. 'Kinsmen!' she said, turning pale. 'When the Prince Abou Abdil asked me in marriage, I told you I would not wed but with one of my own faith.'

'She has been turned Turk,' screamed out the ladies. 'She

wants to be a princess, and has turned Turk,' roared the rabbis.

'Well, well,' said Isaac, in rather an appeased tone, 'let us hear what the poor girl has got to say. Do you want to marry his Royal Highness, Rebecca? Say the word, yes or no.'

Another groan burst from the rabbis – they cried, shrieked, chattered, gesticulated, furious to lose such a prize; as were the women, that she should reign over them, a second Esther.

'Silence,' cried out Isaac, 'let the girl speak – speak boldly, Rebecca dear, there's a good girl.'

Rebecca was as pale as a stone. She folded her arms on her breast and felt the ring there. She looked round all the assembly, and then at Isaac. 'Father,' she said, in a thrilling low steady voice, 'I am not of your religion – I am not of the Prince Boabdil's religion – I… I am of *his* religion.'

'His! Whose? In the name of Moses, girl,' cried Isaac.

Rebecca clasped her hands on her beating chest, and looked round with dauntless eyes. 'Of his,' she said, 'who saved my life and your honour – of my dear, dear champion's. I never can be his, but I will be no other's. Give my money to my kinsmen: it is that they long for. Take the dross, Simeon and Solomon, Jonah and Jochanan, and divide it among you, and leave me. I will never be yours, I tell you, never. Do you think, after knowing him and hearing him speak – after watching him wounded on his pillow, and glorious in battle' (her eyes melted and kindled again as she spoke these words), 'I can mate with such as *you*? Go. Leave me to myself. I am none of yours. I love him, I love him. Fate divides us – long, long miles separate us, and I know we may never meet again. But I love and

83

bless him always. Yes, always. My prayers are his, my faith is his. Yes, my faith is your faith, Wilfrid, Wilfrid! I have no kindred more – I am a Christian!...'

At this last word there was such a row in the assembly as my feeble pen would in vain endeavour to depict. Old Isaac staggered back in a fit, and nobody took the least notice of him. Groans, curses, yells of men, shrieks of women filled the room with such a furious jabbering as might have appalled any heart less stout than Rebecca's. But that brave woman was prepared for all, expecting, and perhaps hoping, that death would be her instant lot. There was but one creature who pitied her, and that was her cousin and father's clerk, Ben Davids, who was but thirteen, and had only just begun to carry a bag, and whose crying and boohooing, as she finished speaking, was drowned in the screams and maledictions of the elder Israelites. Ben Davids was madly in love with his cousin (as boys often are with such ladies of twice their age), and he had presence of mind suddenly to knock over the large brazen lamp on the table, which illuminated the angry conclave, and whispering to Rebecca to go up to her own room and lock herself in, or they would kill her else, he took her hand and led her out.

From that day she disappeared from among her people. The poor and the wretched missed her, and asked for her in vain. Had any violence been done to her, the poorer Jews would have risen and put all Isaac's family to death; and besides, her old flame, Prince Boabdil, would have also been exceedingly wrathful. She was not killed then, but, so to speak, buried alive, and locked up in Isaac's back kitchen; an apartment into which scarcely any light entered, and where she was fed upon scanty portions of the most mouldy bread and water. Little Ben Davids was the only person who visited her, and her sole consolation was to talk to him about Ivanhoe, and how good and how gentle he was, how brave and how true; and how he slew the tremendous knight of the Templars, and how he married a lady whom Rebecca scarcely thought worthy of him, but with whom she prayed he might be happy; and of what colour his eyes were, and what were the arms on his shield, viz. a tree with the word 'Desdichado' written underneath, etc. etc. etc. All which talk would not have interested little Davids, had it come from anybody else's mouth, but to which he never tired of listening as it fell from her sweet lips.

So, in fact, when old Isaac of York came to negotiate with Don Beltran de Cuchilla for the ransom of the Alfaqui's daughter of Xixona, our dearest Rebecca was no more dead than you and I, and it was in his rage and fury against Ivanhoe that Isaac told that cavalier the falsehood which caused the knight so much pain and such a prodigious deal of bloodshed to the Moors – and who knows, trivial as it may seem, whether it was not that very circumstance which caused the destruction in Spain of the Moorish power?

Although Isaac, we may be sure, never told his daughter that Ivanhoe had cast up again, yet Master Ben Davids did, who heard it from his employer; and he saved Rebecca's life by communicating the intelligence, for the poor thing would have infallibly perished but for this good news. She had now been in prison four years three months and twenty-four days, during which time she had partaken of nothing but bread and water (except such occasional titbits as Davids could bring her – and these were few indeed, for old Isaac was always a curmudgeon, and seldom had more than a pair of eggs for his own and Davids' dinner); and she was languishing away when the news came suddenly to revive her. Then, though in the darkness you could not see her cheeks, they began to bloom again: then her heart began to beat and her blood to flow, and she kissed the ring on her neck a thousand times a day at least; and her constant question was, 'Ben Davids! Ben Davids! When is *he* coming to besiege Valencia?' She knew he would come, and indeed, the Christians were encamped before the town ere a month was over.

And now, my dear boys and girls, I think I perceive behind that dark scene of the back kitchen (which is just a simple flat, painted stone-colour that shifts in a minute) bright streaks of light flashing out, as though they were preparing a most brilliant, gorgeous, and altogether dazzling illumination, with effects never before attempted on any stage. Yes, the fairy in the pretty pink tights and spangled muslin is getting into the brilliant revolving chariot of the realms of bliss. Yes, most of the fiddlers and trumpeters have gone round from the orchestra to join in the grand triumphal procession, where the whole strength of the company is already assembled, arrayed in costumes of Moorish and Christian chivalry, to celebrate the 'Terrible Escalade', the 'Rescue of Virtuous Innocence', the 'Grand Entry of the Christians into Valencia', 'Appearance of the Fairy Day-Star', and 'Unexampled displays of pyrotechnic festivity.' Do you not, I say, perceive that we are come to the end of our history, and, after a quantity of rapid and terrific fighting, brilliant change of scenery, and songs, appropriate or otherwise, are bringing our hero and heroine together? Who wants a long scene at the last? Mammas are putting the girls' cloaks and boas on – papas have gone to look for the carriage, and left the box-door swinging open, and letting in the cold air – if there *were* any stage conversation, you could not hear it, for the scuffling of the people who are leaving the pit. See, the orange-women are preparing to retire. Tomorrow their playbills will be as so much waste paper – so will some of our masterpieces, woe is me – but lo! here we come to scene the last, and Valencia is besieged and captured by the Christians.

Who is the first on the wall, and who hurls down the green standard of the Prophet? Who chops off the head of the Emir Abou Whatdyecallem, just as the latter has cut over the cruel Don Beltran de Cuchilla y etc.? Who, attracted to the Jewish quarter by the shrieks of the inhabitants who are being slain by the Moorish soldiery, and by a little boy by the name of Ben Davids, who recognises the knight by his shield, finds Isaac of York *égorgé* on a threshold, and clasping a large back-kitchen key? Who, but Ivanhoe – who but Wilfrid? 'An Ivanhoe to the rescue,' he bellows out; he has heard that news from little Ben Davids that makes him sing. And who is it that comes out of the house – trembling – panting – with her arms out – in a white dress – with her hair down – who is it but dear Rebecca! Look, they rush together, and Master Wamba is waving an immense banner over them, and knocks down a circumambient Jew with a ham, which he happens to have in his pocket... As for Rebecca, now her head is laid upon Ivanhoe's heart. I shall not ask to hear what she is whispering, or describe further that scene of meeting, though I declare I am quite affected when I think of it. Indeed I have thought of it any time these five and twenty years – ever since, as a boy at school, I commenced the noble study of novels – ever since the day when, lying on sunny slopes of half-holidays, the fair chivalrous figures and beautiful shapes of knights and ladies were visible to me – ever since I grew to love Rebecca, that sweetest creature of the poet's fancy, and longed to see her righted.

That she and Ivanhoe were married follows of course, for Rowena's promise extorted from him was that he would never wed a Jewess, and a better Christian than Rebecca now was never said her Catechism. Married I am sure they were, and adopted little Cedric; but I don't think they had any other children, or were subsequently very boisterously happy. Of some sort of happiness melancholy is a characteristic, and I think these were a solemn pair, and died rather early.

William Makepeace Thackeray was born in Calcutta in 1811, the only son of Richmond Thackeray, who worked for the East India Company. His father died when he was three, and he came to England at the age of six to join his remarried mother. Schooled at Charterhouse, Thackeray later studied at Trinity College, Cambridge, where he befriended the eccentric poet Edward Fitzgerald, before a winter in Weimar, Germany, where he met Johann Wolfgang von Goethe. Intended for the law, Thackeray defected to journalism, contributing variously to the *Constitutional*, *Fraser's Magazine*, the *New Monthly Magazine*, and the *Morning Chronicle*. He moved to Paris in 1833, having lost much of his inheritance after the collapse of a Calcutta agency, and in 1836 he married Isabella Shawe, who, after the birth of three children (one of whom died) suffered a permanent mental breakdown in 1840.

It was in the 1840s that Thackeray made his name as an author, with *The Yellowplush Papers* – his social satire from the perspective of a footman – appearing in volume form in 1841. Thackeray's pseudonym, Michael Angelo Titmarsh, became familiar in the early 1840s with *The Great Hoggarty Diamond* and *The Paris Sketch Book*. In 1843 he reverted to 'George Savage FitzBoodle' for *The FitzBoodle Papers*, and eventually took to using his own name a year after his first contributions (caricatures, articles and sketches) appeared in *Punch* magazine.

Vanity Fair, Thackeray's ingenious social satire with its wicked heroine Becky Sharp a mirror for widespread societal hypocrisies, began to appear in monthly numbers in 1847. *The History of Pendennis* (1848–50) followed, again contrasting virtue and villainy, with *The History of Henry Esmond* (1852) and *The Newcomes* (1853–55) expanding upon moral questions raised by various social scenarios. Thackeray continued his lighter work in tandem with his great novels and, in 1861, became the first editor of *Cornhill* magazine, in which he serialised his later work. He died on Christmas Eve, 1863. The scourge of snobs and facile social codes, Thackeray peopled a unique fictional world, a world without heroes, in which foibles and instincts determine character more than principles.

HESPERUS PRESS – 100 PAGES

Hesperus Press, as suggested by the Latin motto, is committed to bringing near what is far – far both in space and time. Works written by the greatest authors, and unjustly neglected or simply little known in the English-speaking world, are made accessible through new translations and a completely fresh editorial approach. Through these short classic works, each little more than 100 pages in length, the reader will be introduced to the greatest writers from all times and all cultures.

For more information on Hesperus Press, please visit our website: **www.hesperuspress.com**

To place an order, please contact:
Grantham Book Services
Isaac Newton Way
Alma Park Industrial Estate
Grantham
Lincolnshire NG31 9SD
Tel: +44 (0) 1476 541080
Fax: +44 (0) 1476 541061
Email: orders@gbs.tbs-ltd.co.uk

SELECTED TITLES FROM HESPERUS PRESS

Gustave Flaubert *Memoirs of a Madman*

Alexander Pope *Scriblerus*

Ugo Foscolo *Last Letters of Jacopo Ortis*

Anton Chekhov *The Story of a Nobody*

Joseph von Eichendorff *Life of a Good-for-nothing*

Mark Twain *The Diary of Adam and Eve*

Giovanni Boccaccio *Life of Dante*

Victor Hugo *The Last Day of a Condemned Man*

Joseph Conrad *Heart of Darkness*

Edgar Allan Poe *Eureka*

Emile Zola *For a Night of Love*

Daniel Defoe *The King of Pirates*

Giacomo Leopardi *Thoughts*

Nikolai Gogol *The Squabble*

Franz Kafka *Metamorphosis*

Herman Melville *The Enchanted Isles*

Leonardo da Vinci *Prophecies*

Charles Baudelaire *On Wine and Hashish*

Wilkie Collins *Who Killed Zebedee?*

Théophile Gautier *The Jinx*

Charles Dickens *The Haunted House*

Luigi Pirandello *Loveless Love*

Fyodor Dostoevsky *Poor People*

E.T.A. Hoffmann *Mademoiselle de Scudéri*

Henry James *In the Cage*

Francesco Petrarch *My Secret Book*

D.H. Lawrence *The Fox*

Percy Bysshe Shelley *Zastrozzi*